Felix Jones
And
The Book
Of
Words

A Felix Jones Adventure

Julian Roderick

Copyright © 2015 Julian Roderick

ISBN: 978-1-326-32338-7

PublishNation, London
www.publishnation.co.uk

For Tom and Matt who wanted an adventure!

Thank you to Victoria for listening when she would rather be watching stuff about vampires.

Huge thanks to my little sister Claire for reading these stories first and, as always, being annoyingly right with her suggestions!

1

Thick black smoke engulfed the far end of the school field like a heavy woollen blanket. Queen Anne's School had been an oasis of calm amongst the hustle and bustle of London life since 1705. The old red brick buildings sat surrounded by acres of green fields and small woods. This was definitely not about to be a day like any other. This Geography lesson wasn't going to end with one of The Sheriff's usual corny jokes from the last century.

The Sheriff, whose real name was Mr Law, had taught Geography at Queen Anne's School since, well, no one could remember. He had taught Felix's father, and Felix's grandfather, and he still used the same lessons and jokes. He was a giant of a man, well over six foot tall, with a grey droopy moustache and a mop of silver curly hair. He wore the same clothes every day, grey trousers, scruffy brown shoes, a white shirt and a tweed jacket with leather elbow patches. The only thing that changed was his tie! All the students thought he lived in the large store cupboard at the front of G11, his Geography Room, where no person, not even the Headmaster, dared to tread.

Whenever a student asked a question The Sheriff would smile and with his loud booming voice announce, "Let's consult the book of words." He would disappear into his storeroom for a few moments before reappearing and entertaining the class, enthralling them with his knowledge and explanation. Even when things broke down, cars, projectors, computers, you would hear, "Let's consult the book of words." After disappearing round a corner he would return and fix the problem with ease. Everyone thought the book of words was his old fashioned way of saying text book or instruction booklet. Today Felix would find out the truth.

The large explosion near the school had stopped the lesson dead in its tracks. The whole class clambered over the wooden desks and chairs to stare out of the windows at the back of the room. They had a fantastic view from the first floor through the floor to ceiling windows that led to a small balcony. The blazing inferno engulfed the large detached house on the edge of the school field that had been empty for as long as the students could remember. The thick black smoke rolled across the muddy pitches towards the captivated audience. The smell of burning filled their nostrils as they excitedly watched the unfolding scene.

Felix turned around and saw The Sherriff stumbling backwards towards the store room. He was as white as a sheet. Felix had never seen the old man this worried. He pulled at Tom's sleeve and the pair crept towards the storeroom. The Sheriff was in there whispering to a tatty old book, it was small enough to fit in a pocket. He was definitely asking lots of questions, the boys strained to listen to the Sheriff but the shrieks of excitement from their classmates drowned out his whispering voice. The old man opened the top drawer in an old oak map cupboard and to the boys' surprise he pulled out a large silver broad sword. The blade was gleaming in the light, the hilt was bedecked with red and blue gemstones. He placed the heavy weapon under his jacket to try and conceal it from his students.

The Sheriff looked up and saw two scared faces peering round the doorway at him. He hurriedly summoned the boys into the room, he was gripping the book as if his life depended on it. As they drew nearer Felix, the shorter of the two, could see the title of the book. He nudged Tom and pointed.

"Look! It's actually real."

Tom brushed his dark mop like fringe away from his eyes and laughed. The ancient myth of The Sheriff and his secret book was true. On the front cover the stunned pair saw in large, old fashioned gold lettering The Book of Words.

"Felix," The Sheriff whispered nervously. "This is yours to keep safe now. Make sure nothing happens to it."

"Eh!" Felix turned to Tom for reassurance. Tom shrugged his shoulders.

"You have been named as The Keeper of the Book. Look!" said the Sheriff as he pointed at the peeling leather surrounding the book.

Felix turned the front of the Book towards him and there under the title he saw

The Keeper
Felix Jones

"The Keeper of this old thing." Tom giggled at the thought of Felix being in charge of anything.

"This is serious," shouted The Sheriff. "Don't let them get hold of it, whatever you do."

"Who? Why?" Felix was getting very confused at The Sheriff's ramblings.

"And why him?" added Tom, "Why not me?" he said as he lifted his arms up flexing his muscles. "I'm the strongest."

"The Book has named Felix, nothing can change that." The Sheriff looked increasingly worried.

"What does the Book do? Why does it need looking after?" Felix was thinking the old man had finally lost the plot.

"You will figure it out in your own time." The Sheriff whispered with a reassuring wink and with that he ushered the boys back into the chaos of the classroom. He then waved, signalling for Felix and Tom to re-join their classmates to watch the ongoing spectacle unravel.

2

The menacing smoke billowed slowly towards the school building, the football goals disappeared into the murky black mass. The tips of the rugby posts looked like mountain peaks poking out above the clouds. The green grass turned grey as the smoke advanced.   Out of the increasing gloom four ghostly figures strode purposely. They were dressed from head to toe in brown leather. Their monks' cloaks added menace to their appearance. They drew long silver swords from under their cloaks and pointed straight towards the balcony of Room G11. The air of excitement and anticipation in the classroom turned to an atmosphere of fear as the monks began to speed up the gentle slope towards the school. The Sheriff, as if knowing what was about to happen, boomed, "Go quietly to the school hall and wait for me there."

Everyone but Felix and Tom rushed towards the door. Tables and chairs flew everywhere as the terrified students fled through the small doorway and into the long corridor. Felix approached The Sheriff.

"Let's get out of here," shouted Tom as the monks climbed onto the balcony.

"Sir, what do I do?" Felix asked, expecting some long helpful answer whilst he held out his hand, signalling Tom to wait.

"You'll figure it out, as we all have," repeated The Sheriff.

There was an almighty crash as one of the monks flew through the window. Shards of glass sprayed over the room. Felix and Tom threw both their hands in front of their faces for protection. The monks stood in a line facing The Sheriff with their swords ready to attack. The petrified boys cowered in the doorway hiding from view behind a toppled desk.

The Sheriff drew his thick gleaming silver sword. He glanced towards his panicking students. He mouthed, "Run." Without a second thought the boys were off down the corridor. Behind them they heard a low, gravelly voice.

"Keeper, where is the Book?" The monk sounded menacing.

"I am no longer The Keeper!" The Sheriff shouted at the intruders.

"What the hell's going on?" Tom screamed at Felix as they run away from the Geography classroom.

"Not a clue! Quick down here." Felix tugged on Tom's blazer as he slid round the corner.

All they heard after that was the crash of swords as the monks attacked. Then a deathly silence fell.

The boys ran as fast as they could to find safety. Tom was a sports star at school so he was way in front of Felix who was always the last to be picked for football. They ran past many classrooms filled with students pressed against the window watching the fire in the old house. Tom shoved open the door to the boys' toilets and dived in, waiting for his best friend to catch him up. The pair had been inseparable since nursery school and had been in many scrapes, but nothing like this. Without a word he pulled Felix through the entrance and into a cubicle, locked the door and slumped against it making sure it could not be opened. Felix held the Book in his hands. He wondered what was so important about this funny little book that he would quite happily have thrown into the school skip.

"What's so special about this?" whispered Tom, snatching the Book from Felix's hand.

"I know as much as you! Mr Law had been The Keeper and now I am." Felix stared at The Book of Words in a state of utter confusion.

Felix was a little confused to say the least, and his eyes began to fill with tears. Tom put his reassuring arms round his friend's shoulders. "Chuck it out of the window, there's a skip down there."

Felix had never disobeyed instructions from a teacher, but this was the first time he felt he might.

"The Sheriff said I had to keep it safe." Felix quivered with fear.

"They don't know you have it," stated Tom. "We'll be fine in here."

Felix thought they would be safe for now – those monsters did not have a clue he was the Keeper so both he and Tom assumed they would be safe from their evil clutches.

A cold shiver ran down his spine as he heard that same low, gravelly voice cry out along the corridor, "The Keeper, Felix Jones. Where are you?"

"You're dead!" Tom murmured to Felix.

"Thanks mate!" exclaimed Felix laughing.

The fire siren began to ring, three separate bells. The school was on lock down. Every door would be locked until the police arrived and they had cleared the building of danger and declared it safe. The pair realised that if they stayed where they were behind the cubicle door they may be found by the caretaker. He scoured the corridors for loose students during lock down and they would be taken to the safety of the School Hall. Old Mr Buckley, the jolly caretaker who looked like a smiley gnome, arrived within two minutes.

"Anyone there?" he shouted as he opened the toilet door.

"Me!" cried Felix with a sense of relief.

"Come on sonny, we need to get you to the hall." The old man stood in the doorway scratching his ears and looking quizzically at Felix. Tom followed them quietly.

They quickly moved through the school corridors, checking for more students as they ran. They turned the corner to enter the main reception where they found their path was blocked by four shadowy figures. The boys saw their faces for the first time, half human and half skeleton. They reeled backwards in horror, they were terrified, they could not move. The blood of The Sherriff dripped off the monks' deathly blades as they eyed their next victims.

To Felix's surprise the jolly old caretaker turned to him and whispered, "I am a Guardian. Don't let that book go. Don't let the Brethren get hold of it. Run!" He drew a large sabre from under his old battered donkey jacket and charged at the monks.

"Scarper," he hollered at the boys before engaging the four intruders in battle.

"This day can't get any weirder!" Tom cried as he dragged Felix off towards the History department.

The boys were once again running. Felix was shivering with fear but he could feel hot sweat pouring down his face and back. There was nowhere to hide, the pair just decided to keep running. All the doors were locked, they flew past room after room filled with terrified students hiding under their desks. This was going on too long to be a practice drill and the atmosphere in the school was tense. A door creaked as it was tentatively opened. Mr Taylor, their favourite History teacher and football coach, grabbed Tom by the collar and pulled them both into the apparent safety of his classroom before locking the door behind them.

Felix knew it would only be a matter of time before they would be discovered by the creatures fighting Mr Buckley. Guardians, Keepers, the Brethren - he was clueless as to what it was they had got themselves involved in. People were dying for the Book. One thing Felix had figured out for himself was that The Book of Words was too important for him to let the monks get their hands on.

3

Out of breath and wet through with perspiration, Felix slumped wearily to the floor whilst Tom lifted his hands above his head desperately trying to catch his breath. He had run all over the football and rugby fields without straining himself but this was the first time he had run for his life. Mr Taylor pulled up a chair and heaved Felix onto it. It was soon made very clear to everyone that this was not a drill. The blood splatters on the boys' shirts pointed to the fact that something horrific was happening out there in the school corridors. Some students, quiet until now, started screaming. Felix thought for a second and cried, "Get out. Use the windows. They're not after any of you."

They did not need telling twice. The class opened the windows and began diving out onto the field and fleeing towards the police car that had screeched down the school drive through the fast dispersing smoke.

A very worried and ashen faced Mr Taylor asked, "What the hell is going on Jones?"

"I don't -," Felix stuttered before he was rudely interrupted.

"And don't say you don't know! What class are you supposed to be in?"

"Mr Law's, sir." Felix was trying his best to be polite.

"Where is Mr Law? Where is Mr Buckley? He should have swept you up and taken you to the hall," asked an increasingly angry Mr Taylor.

"The Brethren got them. I think they're dead. Mr Law was The Keeper and Mr Buckley was The Guardian. He tried to fight them off." Tom knew his answer sounded unbelievable.

"What utter rubbish! What have you done Matthews?" Mr Taylor shouted accusingly.

"Nothing, sir, honestly. There are these monsters, and they came out of the smoke and killed The Sheriff," pleaded Tom, knowing how stupid he sounded. His previous behaviour record in school was a long list of various misdemeanours, and because of this his word was not exactly accepted by the teachers at his school.

Before Mr Taylor could utter another word, a low, gravelly voice boomed along the corridor. "The Keeper. Felix Jones, where are you?" Mr Taylor eyed the window, planning his escape, but his instinct was to protect the boys. As his students he had a duty to ensure they were safe. The wooden frame disintegrated into splinters as the door burst open. The grotesque face of a Brethren monk peered through the gaping doorway into the classroom. For a big man, Mr Taylor had a very high pitched scream. He leapt like an Olympic gymnast straight out of the window onto the school field and ran towards the group of students like a gazelle evading a cheetah.

The boys were left alone to face the four hideous, sword wielding monsters. Felix tucked the old book in the inside pocket of his blazer. He did not know how, but he would do his best to stop them getting their hands on the strange treasure. He wondered if they would kill him for the Book. Why did they want it? It must have some use - but finding out could wait until he had escaped from the room. To his surprise the monks put their swords away. Felix felt a little safer - but not much.
"Scared are you?" shouted Tom, who by this time was waving a chair round his head as a weapon.
Their leader growled, "Are you Felix Jones? Are you The Keeper?"
"No, I'm the man in the moon!" said Tom cockily.
"Enough of this!" screeched the monk. "You are coming with us and so is the Book".

"No we're not." Tom moved in front of Felix. Tom had always protected Felix and this appeared to be no exception. Felix could tell Tom was terrified but just like on the rugby pitch he would not show any weakness. Felix on the other hand was visibly shaking like a leaf.

As the brains of the outfit Felix quickly realised that the monks obviously needed the Keeper as well as the Book for whatever their scheme was. The Brethren would take him alive but he did not fancy a trip into whatever world had spewed forth these strange creatures. His only option was to try to escape and hope he could lose them in the rabbit warren of school corridors.

Tom whispered in Felix's ear, "Right Mr Keeper, how the hell do we get out of this one?"

They were surrounded. There was no easy escape route, the window was blocked by a grinning monk, as was the doorway.

"Geronimo move," Tom screamed at Felix.

"What?" replied Felix as they were being cornered by the monks.

Then he remembered the moves from rugby training the previous night. He winked at Tom and charged at the monk blocking the door, Tom slotted in behind him.

The noise Felix made as he bounced off the monk's iron-like muscles was like a deflating balloon. He fell back against Tom and they both crashed into the poster covered wall. The room started to spin. They felt like they were flying. Their minds went blank and they passed out.

4

As he woke up, Felix asked himself whether he was dead or alive. He could not figure out if he was going upwards, downwards, forwards, backwards, left or right. All he knew was that he felt really sick and that he was travelling at some speed. To feel sick you have to be alive Felix thought. Although the full English breakfast he'd eaten now seemed like a really bad mistake, as his stomach was spinning like a washing machine. The last thing he remembered was bouncing off the monk back into Tom and into the wall of the History classroom and after that, nothing.

"Kidnapped, that's it," he said to himself. "A mad dream? A nightmare?" Felix could not figure out what was happening. He could move his arms and legs, so the monks hadn't tied him up. He could hear nothing apart from the whooshing of the wind as he sped through the air. He was definitely moving, it was no dream. A panicky thought ran through his mind, "The Book of Words!" he cried out. He reached hurriedly inside his school blazer. The Book was still there, tucked safely into his pocket. The monks would have taken the Book to keep it secure if he had been captured. Something else was happening - he was still free!

Felix could not feel anything solid around him. His heart sank as he realised that he would have to open his eyes to find out if he was definitely flying. But what new horrors would he see?

A familiar friendly voice hit his ears, "You OK mate?"

Bravely Felix dared to open his eyes. He looked up and there was Tom beaming from ear to ear.

"Just lie back and enjoy the ride," said Felix's best friend through his giggles.

"Are we dead?" Felix was aching all over.

"We're breathing and talking so I guess not." Tom was always able to lighten the mood.

The bright multi-coloured rays of light burned Felix's eyes. Every colour that existed, in reality or imagination, streamed passed him, making Felix feel dizzy as well as sick. The colours twirled around him - they were in some kind of vortex. He gained his balance and the dizziness calmed. This was the strangest event Felix had ever experienced. He thought they may have sedated him with tranquilisers, like the lion in Madagascar - but there was no music or carnival in his head. Then he saw something strange. Felix was catching glimpses of black and white images in amongst the swirling colours. He tried hard to focus on them. He thought he saw his parents whizz past. Then he caught glimpses of people and places he recognised.

He was dead. This was his life flying before his eyes. Felix had always thought that was a myth. But he could not be dead, he was breathing. He was speaking to Tom. Felix pinched himself to make sure. He was still feeling really sick. Felix concentrated hard, he needed to figure this out, and quickly.

He squinted his eyes tightly in order to see the images clearly: cavemen, Vikings, cowboys, Queen Victoria, Winston Churchill, men in trenches – they all appeared before him. Churches, volcanoes, factories, towns on fire, Roman soldiers, dinosaurs and then Egyptians came next. Then a shiver flowed down his spine as he spotted some monks. Thank goodness they were peaceful monks in a field farming. But he couldn't get those scary half human creatures out of his mind. He knew he had to try and stay away from them and keep the book with him.

So many questions, so few answers. He became frustrated and more confused as he filled his head with all sorts of possible theories. He slapped himself hard across the face as he remembered the last words of The Sheriff. "You will figure it out as we all have". He wondered whether the monks had really killed The Sheriff and Mr Buckley. The blood on his shirt said most probably.

"This is the best History lesson ever." Tom was grinning from ear to ear.

"Where are we? What's happening?" Felix had never been as scared in his life.

"It's like Doctor Who!" said Tom, "God knows what it is but we can't do anything until it stops."

"What if they're at the end?" Felix dreaded the thought of having to face those monsters again.

"Then we'll probably die," replied Tom with a smile. He could always be relied upon to be calm in a crisis.

"This must have happened to The Sheriff and the other Keepers in the past," said Felix. "I want to know how long the Brethren have been after this battered old book."

"Enough of the questions!" shouted Tom. "Remember what The Sheriff said, 'figure it out as you go along'."

The images kept flashing amongst the coloured lights: the Twin Towers, doctors operating, boats, planes, animals, rainforests, works of art, Florence Nightingale - the entertainment went on for what seemed like an eternity.

Their journey came to an abrupt end as they hit the floor with an almighty thump. Felix ached all over. Dazed he shook his head from side to side. It was all a weird dream, he had been knocked out when he hit the wall! A feeling of relief momentarily washed through him.

15

"The monks!" he quietly whimpered. If it was a dream they would be waiting, waiting to take him somewhere he did not want to go.

"They're not here!" Tom announced confidently as he lay on his back wondering where they had ended up.

It was cold, the wind whistled above them and the ground felt soft like sand. In the distance a strange rumble of engines could be heard above the crashing of waves. This was most definitely not a History room! Looking up through the tall wispy grass swaying back and forth in the building wind there was a sudden realisation they had been here before.

"This is marram grass," said Felix.

"What? How do you remember this stuff?" Felix, to Tom's annoyance had always been the brains of the outfit.

This was marram grass. They were on a sand dune like the ones they had visited with the school in Year 7 on the Geography trip.

"This can't be Dawlish Warren!" exclaimed Tom. He did not realise that he wasn't far from his imagined destination.

It was dawn, the gentle heat of the rising sun warmed their faces as they lay still in shock.

"Devon? Devon?" Felix whispered. "How the hell have we got from London to Devon?"

He reached for his mobile phone and dialled his father. He would come and pick them up. It would take some explaining though. All he got was silence! He checked the signal bars, none. "Typical!" he thought "Lost, alone and no signal." He dabbed the Facebook icon on his smart phone - *no internet connection* came the message. He lay there thinking that he was sure he texted his mother from there last year.

"Try yours!" Tom did but the result was the same.

"Trust you to bring me to the only place without any signal." Tom was holding his phone out in every direction searching for a connection.

"I didn't bring you anywhere," retorted Felix.

The argument was interrupted by an ear shattering explosion. They were covered in flying sand and vegetation. A second explosion and a third followed quickly until they lost count. The boys had to move before a bomb landed on them. They had obviously been dumped on the army training ground they had been warned away from the previous summer.

For the second time that day Tom stated, "You're going to die." He lay there laughing.

Felix raised his head above the long grass and looked at the devastation around them. Craters and smoke were everywhere. He had completely forgotten about the journey and the Brethren. They had to get out of there. He hit the deck when he heard bullets flying past his ears. The firing ceased and there was shouting, lots of shouting, in a strange language.

"What the hell is happening now?" Tom lay on his stomach, too scared to move.

He peered through the grass out to sea. Tom could not believe his eyes, a beach covered in concrete, barbed wire and wooden structures, and beyond them boats as far as he could see. This was a huge army exercise, he thought. He was grabbed by the scruff of his neck and pulled to his feet. "Nooooooooooo," he screamed, thinking the monks had got him.

The man in the blue uniform that appeared in front of him did not ease his feeling of dread.

5

The sight of the soldier put their brains into overdrive. They both knew they had seen the uniform before. The language, the uniform, the bombs. The lightbulb ignited.

"Germans!" they both whispered together.

"I hope this is one of those games people do on a weekend." Tom looked as if he was praying as the bombs continued to rain down around them.

"I don't think so, this is for real," squealed Felix.

This was without doubt no army exercise in Devon. The boys knew enough history to realise that they had to be on the other side of the English Channel! They turned towards the beach, the boats were getting closer. The barrage of explosions increased and gunfire once more began to fly over their heads.

"How did we get to be part of D-day?" shouted Felix above the noise. "It's impossible!" Felix shook his head in disbelief, still not quite knowing how he had travelled back in time over 70 years.

"Doctor Who," screamed a startled Tom, "I told you - like Doctor Who!"

They were dragged away from the dunes and inland towards a village. The Germans were taking them to safety. The buildings were strange and multi-coloured. Those that were still standing after the bombing had steep roofs made of old terracotta tiles. The roads were filled with jeeps and rifle wielding Germans running frantically towards the beach to repel the impending surprise attack. This was real. A farmhouse to their right disintegrated as another shell hit, throwing the boys and their rescuer into the roadside ditch. Muddy, stinking of stagnant water and terrified, Felix clambered out and grabbed Tom. They ran as quickly as they could towards the nearby village leaving the German motionless in the ditch.

There was nobody to be seen, the locals must have fled a long time ago. They took refuge behind what was left of an old stone wall. Breathing deeply they took stock of their surroundings. The sign on the wall read 'Colleville-sur-mer', a familiar name to Felix. He wracked his memory for information. He had heard the name in one of Mr Taylor's History lessons. It was one of the first villages captured by the forces who landed on Sword Beach, Normandy. Captured within an hour following intense fierce fighting, it had been flattened by the Allies. Although gladdened by the thought that he was within an hour of meeting some friendly forces, he was also sure that if he stayed in the village he would be blown to smithereens.

"We have to move." Felix insisted.

"No we don't, the British will be here and we will be saved," snarled Tom.

"Numpty! We'll be in Britain in 1944. We need to get further away and figure this out." Felix ordered with an air of authority.

The noise and dust was unbearable, they could not stay here. They had to move inland away from the battle. They could not quite believe that they had travelled back through time, and still held on to the hope that this might be a very realistic re-enactment, but the screams and persistent noise of machine gun fire coming from the beach convinced them. Once again they were running for their lives.

6

In floods of tears Felix ran down the gravel road desperately trying to keep up with Tom. They eventually came to a bridge over a river. They could still hear the deafening sounds of the battle on the beach and feel the ground rumble and shake with every bomb that fell. They crawled under the bridge and found a well camouflaged alcove to rest inside.

The Sheriff's words "You'll figure it out like all of us did," echoed in Felix's head. Figure it out, he thought angrily.

"Why won't somebody just tell me what's going on?" he screamed up at the bridge.

Well it was not going to happen unless he opened 'The Book of Words'. Wearily, he pulled the tatty old book out of his blazer and stared in wonder at it. There on the cover was his name:

The Book 0f Words

The Keeper

Felix Jones

"Right, I know this. I am The Keeper. The Brethren want the book I'm supposed to be keeping safe, and there are Guardians who will protect me. But where are the Guardians? And who are they?" "Talking to myself - the first sign of madness!" he thought, chuckling.

Tom piped up, "Me, you muppet! I'll protect you like I've always done."

"I know but this is way beyond a scrap at break time." Felix knew he could always rely on Tom.

"What's the Book about anyway?" asked Tom.

"Not a clue, I haven't had a chance to read any of it yet if you hadn't noticed!" Felix screamed at him.

The Book had been his for what seemed like forever and its contents were still a mystery. With great trepidation he pulled up the leather cover to reveal the first page. It read:

Location: Normandy, France

Date: 6th June 1944

Languages: French and German

Then there was a map of the local area and a small map of France dated 1944.

"What does it say?" asked his anxious friend, hoping for a way out of all of this to be revealed.

Felix showed him the page.

"It's blank!" screamed Tom, "Great, we're looking after an old blank note book."

"Can't you see it?" laughed Felix, realising that maybe only The Keeper could read The Book of Words. He told Tom what the page said.

"Great, a mystical A-Z!" Tom put his head in his hands, accepting that he was deep in something he did not understand and could not control.

"There must be more to this than telling me where I am." Felix could see Tom was becoming increasingly worried. The second page had at some point in the past been torn out. Page after page was blank until he found a huge description and explanation of what was happening in that area, and what was about to occur. The Book could tell the future or the past – well, it depended on your point of view, and where and when you had come from. He told Tom what he had discovered and they agreed that this could be very handy. Felix read on.

Another run was on the cards as the Book described a bit of a stalemate in this area for a few days, with hand to hand combat and feats of bravery by soldiers on both sides. They could not stay here, as all the bridges were to be blown up by retreating German troops to slow down the Allied advance.

"Where are you taking me next then?" Tom sat down throwing stones into the river. Felix didn't answer, but sat staring at the Book in silence. Before long Tom lay back and was snoring like a pig.

Felix knew they had to leave, running was again a certainty. The next explosion made Felix drop the Book - it fell open at its final pages. There he could see two lists of names. At the bottom of the first list he saw his name:

Felix Jones   2015 – present

The list went back to the date 476. This had been going on for centuries. There were all sorts of names from all sorts of languages on here. The Sheriff sat above his name:

Trevor Law   1944 – 2015 deceased

Everybody above him was deceased. The memory of the Brethren monks came rushing back. They were running from the war and running from those monsters. He could not decide what he was most scared of. The second list on the last page was an exact duplicate with two omissions. The Sheriff and Felix were missing, the last entry was:

Emile Dupont   1938 – present

According to this list Emile Dupont was still alive. Felix checked the first list again. It stated Emile had died in 1944, the year The Sheriff became the Keeper!

Felix was an intelligent boy, he was one of the top students in his year group and he had come in the top ten in the entrance exam to Queen Anne's School, but this was taking some working out. He made sure the Book was closed and fell into a deep sleep, they had run miles and had had what can only be described as a very stressful day.

The rumbling of a large military vehicle crossing the bridge woke them with a start. The draught caused by the commotion above blew open the Book to the first page. There was an additional entry:

The Keeper: Emile Dupont   Paris, France

Felix now knew his next destination, the French capital. He had to find the other Keeper. He would know what was happening and how to get back home.

"We have to go to Paris," said Felix, after explaining the entry in the book to Tom.

"OK," Tom replied sceptically. "As long as I get home in one piece I don't care."

They had to get to Paris without firstly getting shot by the Germans or the British, and secondly, without bumping in to the Brethren and being dragged off to who knows where. If the Keeper had been present through the ages it stood to reason that the Brethren had been too. Once again they were on the move; but this time was different, they knew where they were going.

7

The destination this time was clear, they were off to Paris. The boys knew they had to head away from the carnage unravelling on the beaches. If they stayed they would be in real danger. They climbed up onto the track and found themselves amidst a column of German vehicles, jeeps and trucks, full of troops heading in the opposite direction to them.

A captain shouted, "You silly boy, find your family and get out of here."

"You don't have to tell me that," Felix replied in perfect German.

The Captain was as shocked as Felix that he could speak in his native tongue. Having only completed a year of French at school, Felix was totally confused by the fact he could now speak fluent German. The Captain stared open mouthed as he disappeared into the distance along the narrow dust covered track.

"Hey genius." Tom was once again grinning, "Since when can you speak German?"

Felix realised it must be the Book. It did say:

Languages: French and German

"I think it's the book," he laughed. "I am Language Man!"

The Book had the power to let the Keeper understand and speak any language he was spoken to in. "This will be handy," thought Felix. He smiled as he accepted he was in the middle of the most exciting adventure. It was highly dangerous but fun. The pair walked passed the soldiers, smiling as they went.

"You're going to get your backsides kicked," Felix quipped to the German column.

"What?" asked Tom.

When Felix translated Tom laughed out loud and repeated the phrase over and over with Felix. The replies they received were not so polite! They were in little danger here as the Germans thought they were French. They looked odd though, dressed from head to toe in clothes that screamed English school children. Felix ran into a farmhouse garden and grabbed some ragged clothes off the washing line for them to wear. They changed in the shed were they also found a collection of work boots.

"Great!" said Tom looking at the clothes. "Can't you do anything right?"

"What?" Felix, who was feeling quite pleased with himself, was becoming annoyed.

"Who's wearing this?" Tom held up a flowery blue dress.

"My hair is too short to be a girl in 1944 and my bum would look big in that," said Felix as he began to laugh. "You'll have to put it on."

They would fit right in looking like a rural farm worker and his big sister. Tom really wanted to dress in a stripy top and beret and ride a bike with a string of onions round his neck, but this did not seem to be the fashion in 1944. A bike would be good right now though to speed up their journey.

The column passed by. Some of the soldiers had thrown them some bread, which the boys gulped down in seconds. They opened the Book and Felix studied the map. Paris was miles away - it would take the pair weeks to walk there. However, something strange had appeared on the map. A red sword flashed in a nearby village. The winding route to the sword was highlighted by a faint yellow line.

"What now? What does this mean?" Felix cried out in despair.

"Please, not so loud. I'm a lady," quipped Tom.

"Do you want me to follow this line?" Felix asked.

"What line?" Tom asked before realising Felix was talking to the Book.

Felix could see words slowly appearing on the page overleaf. The previously blank second page had one word on it:

'Yes'

The Book had answered his question. "How do I get home?" was the next logical enquiry. The page remained blank. The book flew across the road as it was thrown in anger.

"Why won't you answer me?" shouted Felix.

Tom collected the Book, dusted it off and opened it up. He passed it back to his tearful friend and Felix explained how the book had answered some of his questions and not others. Tom turned to the second page where Felix saw a short, sharp answer:

'Ask the right questions.'

A moody, sarcastic Book was all every confused, scared, excited schoolboy needed for company when they had travelled into a time and world they knew little about. The boys were left with little choice; they needed to follow the yellow line. At least they had a mystical sat-nav to help them find their way.

The sound of war became a distant murmur as the friends meandered along the roads highlighted in yellow upon the map. Orchards abundant with ripe, juicy fruit fed their growing hunger. It was a beautiful part of the world with flowers in full bloom and crops ripening for harvest all swaying and rippling in the gentle breeze. It was a shame that in a short time they would be flattened by tanks and the advancing armies of both sides.

They had moved swiftly, picking up drinks of water at village wells and pumps as they passed through. The local people were friendly and as Felix could speak fluent French, thanks to the book, they gave them food, mostly bread and cheese. Madame Burton would be most impressed with the improvement in his language skills. However, none of the phrases he was learning in class about pets were very useful on this journey.

They had walked all day and had almost reached their destination. There was a small hamlet ahead. It was a strange collection of ramshackle buildings around a church with a tall, intricately carved spire.

"That's it," pointed Felix.

"Right come on, let's get this over with." Tom was eager to return home as quickly as possible.

"I'm bushed." Felix let out a large yawn.

The boys were absolutely shattered and decided that they needed to be fully awake and alert before facing what lay waiting for them in the nearby village. Felix still did not know whether the sword indicated danger or help. He wondered whether the Brethren were lying in wait for them. The new day would bring many answers, of that he was sure. The pair buried themselves in a large haystack and were asleep in seconds.

8

"Atchoooo"

Felix's sneeze brought their slumber to an abrupt halt. It took a while for Felix to remember it was not a dream and he really was in Normandy, wearing stolen clothes under a haystack and freezing. The stubbly hay stuck up his nose, the dust blocked his nostrils. The sun was rising and the rays slowly warmed his weary body. He took a mouthful of the French stick he had in his pocket and envisaged what lay ahead. A fight to the death with those freaky faced Brethren monks, another weird instruction from The Book of Words, he just did not know.

"Come on then sleepy head." Tom was sat in the field in his underpants sunbathing. "Let's see if the Brethren hurt girls too." He laughed as he slipped on the flowery dress.

A stone wall skirted the field and led towards the small village they had found the previous evening. The red sword had disappeared from the map, so this must be their destination. They kept low and crawled stealthily alongside the sheltering wall. It was early. Hopefully nobody would be awake. Tom reached the first building. As he peaked over the window sill the curtains opened and a portly woman dressed in her nightclothes shrieked. It was a scream that woke the whole community. Felix dived under a corrugated iron sheet tunnel and Tom hid in a bush. The stench was overwhelming and a warmth told Felix of a presence. He turned around carefully and there was the biggest pig he had ever seen. For the second time in as many seconds a shriek alerted the whole village to their whereabouts. Running was on the cards again. Felix brushed off the mud and fled into a nearby barn where he was soon joined by Tom. They found temporary shelter under a tarpaulin.

Outside the villagers ran round frantically searching high and low for the intruders. Farmers had shotguns, and the women swung rolling pins back and forth looking scarier than the monks. The locals were as frightened as the boys. 'This is ridiculous,' Felix thought. 'There's nothing for anyone to be wary about' and without a care he threw back the covering. Hearing the rustle, the farmers turned, cocked their guns and aimed them at the strange looking boys.

"The British are coming!" Felix shouted excitedly.

The guns were lowered as the men realised the intruders were French.

"Where are you from?" a large scarred man asked.

Although tempted to tell the truth, Felix decided discretion was the better part of valour. Tom for once was keeping his mouth shut and left it to Felix to sort out.

"We're from Colleville-sur-mer, the British have landed and are heading this way."

"Are you sure?"

"Yes, they're pushing the Germans back. My sister and I ran from the bombing," he said pointing at Tom laughing.

"What now?" Tom asked angrily.

"That farmer fancies you," chortled Felix.

The pop of champagne corks stopped the argument and the appearance of the French flags meant party time. After four years of German occupation the villagers would soon be free again. An elderly farmer's wife picked Felix up, hugged him and gave him a smacker of a kiss on the lips. The pair relaxed and joined in the dancing, but the nagging question of the red sword and what it meant swirled through the back of Felix's mind.

A decrepit, hunched, old gentleman appeared from a workshop on crutches.

"What's all this noise?" he growled angrily

"The British are coming" the villagers sang out all at once.

"Thank God for that!" the elderly grouch exclaimed as he stood upright, threw away his crutches and ran towards the gathered celebrating crowd. His accent became less French and more English. The boys smiled at him.

"You English?" he enquired in French.

"You German?" came the sarcastic reply from Felix.

A smile spread slowly across the man's face, but disappeared when Felix spoke again.

"No, I'm pretending to be French too!" announced Felix in English, much to a confused Tom's surprise.

The man looked the pair up and down and said thoughtfully whilst scratching his ears, "I think I've been expecting you."

"How the... oh never mind, it's the Book isn't it?" sighed Felix.

The man nodded gently and led the boys towards his workshop. If he was expecting them it was either going to be a long journey or death. The boys followed slowly and entered a room filled with old metal tools. In the middle of the room was a red hot furnace. The workshop was that of a Blacksmith.

"I've been here three years, helping the French Resistance," the smiling man stated.

"I'm Group Captain Pomeroy of the RAF."

"I'm Tom Matthews of Queen Anne's School sir!" Tom saluted playfully.

"I fear you boys are not here as spies or as British soldiers." The increasingly excited Group Captain stated.

"No, we're here to... well I don't know why we're here!" Felix scratched his head trying to figure out why they were there.

"I don't know why you are here either, but yesterday morning I started to get the signal."

"The signal the invasion was coming?" asked Tom.

"Well, yes. In between all that something more important was happening to me," said their new friend.

The Group Captain delved in a pile of rags behind his anvil and pulled out some more appropriate clothes for Tom. He reached back in and picked up a long object wrapped in an oily blanket. To the boys surprise he unrolled the blanket to reveal a silver sabre. The boys had seen something similar before.

"What is it with all these swords?" asked Tom wearily. "Can't we use machine guns or hand grenades?"

It was identical to the sword Mr Buckley had tried to fight off the monks with.

"You're a Guardian!" whispered Felix.

"Yes Felix, I am. I was looking forward to a nice cup of tea in a china cup whilst I caught up with all the news from home in the Officer's Mess on the beach. The invasion would have brought that tonight or tomorrow."

"Tomorrow," Felix winked.

"That doesn't matter now; my oldest orders take priority. I must guide you in whatever quest you are on and ensure the Book stays with you, or is passed on safely to the next Keeper."

"You wait here. I'll find another Guardian. You need a rest from war." Felix said considerately.

"That cannot be - look at the map. Is there another red sword anywhere near here?"

The map was just a map as far as Felix could see. On a positive note they had company for the rest of the trip to Paris.

"What does a Guardian do?" Tom was just as confused as he had been after the explosion at school.

"How do you become a Guardian?" Felix had heard lots of names but didn't have a clue what they meant.

"How do we get home?" enquired both boys together.

"Enough," snapped the Group Captain, "answers later, now we get to Paris."

"But…," said Felix before he realised he wasn't going to get any joy now.

"Before we leave, I need to send a message." The Guardian dragging a radio out from under a toolbox.

"Broadsword to Danny Boy, Broadsword to Danny Boy"

"Danny Boy to Broadsword, go ahead. Over," came the crackly reply.

"The enemy is east of last, 20 miles, avoid last. Over"

"Understood. Roger and out," the posh English voice disappeared.

As he grabbed a rucksack from under the rags, the Group Commander turned to his new charges and said, "I've had this packed for years and never met a Keeper. These villagers are safe now, so where are our adventures taking us?"

"Paris!" Tom at least knew where they were heading next.

Felix could see the cogs turning in the Group Commanders head.

"Group Commander," said Felix.

"I'm not in the RAF now kid, call me Jack."

Tom laughed at Felix and shouted, "Tally ho old chap, we're in a black and white war film!"

Jack pushed the boys quickly towards the barn. They had not noticed, but the tarpaulin they had hidden under sat next to a motorbike and sidecar. Jack gave Felix his rucksack and his sabre and shoved him into the sidecar.

"On the back," he bellowed at Tom as he started the engine on the old machine, "and hold on tight."

"Merci beaucoup mes amis. Bon chance." Shouted Jack as they sped past the party, which was now in full flow. The villagers all waved and returned the Group Captain's sentiment. The motorbike accelerated and the village was soon a dot on the horizon behind them.

9

The wind blew their hair all over the place. Felix's mother would have a fit if she could see him hurtling along with a complete stranger on a motorbike without a helmet. That would warrant a month's grounding but he had a feeling she would never find out. The French countryside was a blur as Jack twisted the throttle to its absolute limit. After about an hour they came to a stop.

"German checkpoint," whispered Jack.

He turned left down a side track and stopped under a large willow tree next to a river.

"May as well have lunch," he declared as he produced a well packed picnic of French goodies.

"Where do you keep your sword?" Jack asked Felix.

"Behind his left ear!" Tom was giggling again. He found the thought of his little friend wielding a sword hilarious. Tom had been fencing since he was six and knew how to handle a sword.

"What sword?" asked Felix.

"The Keeper's sword, it has been passed down through the ages from Keeper to Keeper." Jack was visibly worried at Felix's lack of a weapon.

"I don't have a sword," Felix whimpered apologetically.

"How long have you been the Keeper?" asked Jack.

"One and a half days!" revealed Tom.

"When the old Keeper gave you the book did he have a sword?"

"A huge one with a jewelled handle?" Felix described the sword The Sheriff had been using.

"Yes, where was it?" asked Jack in a panic.

"Stuck in a monk, I hope," whispered Tom.

"You will need the sword to protect yourself from the Brethren." Jack was getting more and more serious.

"I can't get it now, I don't know how to get back to school." Felix was obviously flustered by his failure to have a sword.

"How do we get back to 2015? How do we get home?" asked an increasingly desperate Tom.

"I have never known how the Book works but I do know a bit about the swords." As they relaxed in the shade of the willow's branches, Jack told the boys all he knew.

"The Book of Words gave advice and knowledge to people in order for society to be fair and equal. The Book was used to show how different peoples could live together in harmony and share all they had for the good of everyone. The Guardians come from a group of knights who vowed to stop the Book getting into the hands of those who would use it selfishly to rule the world. Evil dictators who would enslave populations so that the majority would live to serve the ruling classes and those who would expand their empires until all lay under their rule. The Guardians have protected the Book and the Keeper since the time of that vow during medieval times."

The boys looked at each other in amazement. Jack continued his tale,

"Those that knew of the book split into factions. The Brethren came from an ancient order which has always wanted the power the Book brings. I'm not sure of the details, but in the early sixth century other factions vowed to never let the Brethren get their hands on the Book and a task was set to find the first Keeper. The test was to find a warrior worthy of the honour. Sabres were forged for the Guardian Knights and the weapons were blessed by a Druid. They vowed to pass the sabres on to their first born to carry on protecting the Keeper. The Guardians dispersed to all parts of the kingdom so that The Keeper was safe wherever he went. The Brethren have always had the power to defeat all who come against them, and the

Guardians vowed to give up their lives to the Brethren for the Keeper's safety. The Keeper was given a special sword - the only weapon that could kill one of the Brethren. This too is passed on with the book from Keeper to Keeper. It was the one weapon that could hold back the Brethren. That is all I know of the history of the Book."

"All sounds a bit Harry Potter." Tom was convinced this was a fairy tale

"I didn't believe any of this either," announced Jack. "My father told me this on his deathbed as he passed me the sabre, he said I would know when the Keeper was close."

"How do you know it's true?" Felix for once agreed with Tom.

"My Grandfather had died of a heart attack but nobody remembered seeing him ill in bed or collapsed on the floor. I took a sneaky look inside his coffin before the funeral. He had a massive wound from his stomach to his throat. It was no heart attack that killed him, it was a large blade. It is my turn now, there are hundreds of us to protect you: few of us see action, but this is rather a jolly wheeze."

"Jolly wheeze! We could all die!" exclaimed Felix.

"We've come back to 1944 to spend our last moments with a madman whose sole aim in life is to die protecting you with an old sabre." Tom couldn't believe their luck.

"It's my destiny," Jack announced ironically.

"How the hell is that sabre going to get us through the German lines around Paris? They have machine guns, tanks, planes and bombs - massive bombs!" Tom once again doubted Jack's story.

"It's not the Germans we need to be worried about. As far as they know we're three Frenchies out for a pootle on our motorbike," Jack said with great confidence.

"But…" said Felix.

"No questions, you're the one with the magic book. Get us through the checkpoint." Tom reached over and got the Book out from under Felix's jacket.

Felix opened the Book. "How do I get past the German checkpoint?" The answer appeared.

'You can speak German and French you fool!'

He fell back laughing. "What's so funny?" asked Jack.

Felix showed Jack the page. "Why is a blank page so amusing?" their Guardian asked.

"You had to ask," laughed Tom.

Only Felix could see the answers. He gave the Book to Jack.

"Is this a joke, blank page after blank page," exclaimed Jack.

Tom smiled and turned to Jack, "He's the only one that can see it. I thought he may be nuts until he found you using the invisible map."

Felix suddenly realised that if the Brethren needed the Book they may not be able to access its powers without the help of the Keeper.

"Do you have papers Jack?" asked Felix.

"Yes, of course, standard issue." Jack took some tatty passes from his coat.

"Can you speak French?" added Felix.

"Yes, of course," came the Guardian's reply.

"Just ride up as normal and leave the rest to me." Felix was growing more confident in the power of the Book.

"What about me?" Tom felt left out of the plans.

"You just keep your mouth shut for a change and let me do the talking," answered Felix. For the first time Tom needed Felix to get him out of a spot of bother.

10

The German guards lowered the yellow barrier across their path.

"Papers please," one spat.

Jack handed his forged French passes to the soldier who returned them after a cursory glance.

"And you?" he asked the boys.

"I've lost mine. I'm from Colleville-sur-mer. The British are coming and all our houses are gone," replied Felix in French.

"Rubbish!" shouted the guard.

Felix realised that mobile phones had to wait another 50 years to be invented and communication would be slow. "Radio your men there."

The guard disappeared into the hut. A frantic phone call later, he reappeared ashen faced.

"How do you know this? The battle is still raging."

"I've come from there," Felix nervously replied.

"Lock them up, something is not right!" shouted the guard to his fellow soldier.

Felix thought quickly, "Speak German for God's sake!"

Aloud he barked, "I am General Dietrich von Choltitz's messenger." It was a good job he paid attention in History lessons and could remember the name of the German leader in Paris. "My name is Captain Hans Thatdodishes. I have worked for three years unearthing the French Resistance and have been sent from the front to report to the General in Paris. This peasant and his son had the only working vehicle left in the village. If YOU want to be responsible for the fall of the Third Reich then lock us up."

The soldier saluted gingerly and opened the barrier.

Once again they were on their way. "How did you get out of that? You can speak German?" Jack was amazed at Felix's new found language skills.

"The Book of Words, I'm beginning to like it," giggled Felix, feeling content for the first time in two days

The motorbike began to splutter. Jack shook it and announced that they were out of fuel. Dusk was closing in fast so they wheeled the bike into a roadside hut. Jack disappeared, promising to return with a meal fit for a king. He came back with a can of petrol, some ham, cheese and bread. The boys wondered if the French ate anything else!

"Do you do fencing in school old bean?" Jack asked Felix.

Tom spat out his cheese, "Most schools in the twenty first century don't do fencing," he said. "Felix and sports are relative strangers," he quipped.

"What do young people do for fun then?" asked an exasperated Jack.

"We play games on our laptops and game stations with people all over the world and watch films on Netflix and the telly." replied Felix.

"What language are you speaking?" chortled Jack.

The boys spent the next hour astonishing Jack with tales of technological advances over the coming 70 years. Felix feared that Jack would not witness any of them. "Where are you from?" asked Felix. "London, Kensington. If I die promise me you will get the sword to my son."

"I think the Book will sort it out, but if it doesn't I will," promised Felix.

"Enough of this, plenty of fun to be had yet. Time for a fencing lesson." Jack insisted the boys both joined in. He handed Felix a lump of wood that he could hardly lift, let alone swing around. "Your sword is heavy, get used to fighting with this."

"I've had lessons for years," sniggered Tom. "I go with my dad every week." He grabbed a stick and went off fighting imaginary foes. Felix raised his eyebrows towards Jack and began his first ever fencing lesson.

Within minutes Felix was a sweaty mess as he tried to fend off Jack's attacks. Felix wished he had an instructor like Mr Miyagi. Wax on, wax off was much easier than this!

"You must learn to use less energy. Let the sword swing naturally, don't force it," advised a watching Tom. "Go with it, don't stop it and come back."

"If you know so much you have a go," cried Felix.

"I'm not likely to have to use a sword in anger, am I?" Tom was coming to terms with the fact that he probably would.

"You never know." Jack threw him a branch. "Your turn."

Tom showed his skill and gave Jack a good run for his money. A tired Jack waved for Felix to replace him and the two friends practised together. Then Jack, after catching his breath, replaced Tom. Blows came from every direction raining on Felix. He fended them off with a determination he did not know he possessed; mind you it was a real sabre coming at him at speed. Jack relented and patted Felix on the back, "Well done old man, we'll make a fighter out of you yet."

"A right little Zorro," said Tom, "you'll get better and better."

"You reckon." Felix stifled a yawn.

"Time for sleep, tomorrow could be a long day." Jack pulled some blankets out of his pack.

Felix was feeling guilty, he had dragged a man from the verge of a homecoming into an adventure, which although enjoyable, that would lead to possible oblivion. He was exhausted but he spent the night putting together what he had gleaned about the book. One question still burned brightly. "How in the name of all that is good did we end up in 1944?" Felix asked Tom.

"In the words of The Sheriff, we'll figure it out," he replied with a smile. "Our parents will be frantic. We'll be all over the news. London schoolboys kidnapped by strange creatures. 'Nationwide search brings no results' say confused police."

"They'll never believe the truth," giggled Felix. The pair drifted off to sleep slowly, hoping more answers would be forthcoming tomorrow.

11

"Wakey, wakey young fellows. Time for another lesson," shouted Jack as he banged two iron bars together as an alarm. Surprisingly, it began with a talk on tactics whilst bathing in the nearby stream. The water was clean and refreshing, but freezing. It was so cold that the boys didn't listen to half of the lecture. Felix did remember to never fight angry and defend until the opening comes. Handy advice but could he really kill someone? Then he realised he would probably only be using it against the monks. No problem he was sure he could slice them into pieces.

"How far to Paris?" asked Felix

"Not far now, but we need to hole up and put a plan together before we enter the city. First take this!" Jack's sabre flew towards Felix's head. He rolled on the floor and grabbed his stump of wood. Lesson part two was in session. A few days of practice and they were packing for the ride south to Paris. Holding a large boulder in each arm, Felix felt like an idiot. Apparently this would increase his arm strength and improve his thrust and parry. Tom thought he looked like a prat and laughed as they rode on along the country roads.

Checkpoint after checkpoint were passed with little bother. Columns of German troops flowed north towards Normandy. Waving politely and smiling through gritted teeth they rode without disturbance throughout the morning. They stopped atop a gentle hill for lunch: ham, cheese and bread again. The view was fantastic; the churches and buildings of Paris spread out in the distance, and of course the Eiffel Tower took centre stage. Felix had never seen it; pictures, films yes; but Paris was one place he had not visited. His father had waxed lyrical about rugby tours in his youth and romantic weekends with Felix's mother, and had spent hours showing him photos of drunken escapades with old mates and his mother posing in front of the landmarks. It was a pity his first visit was under such circumstances.

"Where are all the tower blocks?" Tom remembered them from his last visit to Disneyland Paris. His family took great holidays every year whilst Felix enjoyed his camping trips with his parents in the Lake District and Snowdonia.

"Really? Really?" snorted Felix. "They haven't been built yet you muppet!" he laughed out loud. "Where now?" he asked Jack.

"I have a friend in the service living near here," declared Jack, "We can't tell him about the book. He isn't a Guardian. You are now a young tail gunner shot down over northern France, and Tom you are the radio operator of the same Lancaster Bomber. I rescued you last month and your return to Blighty hasn't been organised yet."

"OK, as long as you're sure we'll be safe," said Felix.

"Positive, come on. We're on foot from here." Jack placed his rucksack on his back, his sabre under his long trench coat, and set off down the hill.

An hour later in a suburb of Paris, Jack approached a rickety old black door. A moustached man named Trevor answered and greeted Jack like a long lost son. Introductions were made, food was eaten, and for the first time in a few days Felix and Tom would sleep in their own room on a comfortable bed.

The light was flooding through the closed shutters when Felix awoke. He slowly made his way down the wooden staircase to the dining room. Piled on the table were telephone books and maps. Jack and Tom were ready to make a plan of action. After a breakfast of you can guess what, they began.

It was hopeless, Dupont was one of the most common surnames in France, and there were thousands of Duponts in the Paris books. They had to find another way. 'Of course!' thought Felix, 'The Book!' He opened the Book to the map. It had changed; there was still the map of France, but there was also a street map of Paris. There were three red swords on the map: one on the opposite side of the city, one in the centre near the Montmartre and the last about five streets away. The route to each was marked by a yellow line. Realising nobody else could see the map Felix transferred the locations onto the map laid out on the table. He scoured the book's map for any other clues but there was nothing. If he had the internet he could surf for Duponts in those areas as he supposed one of the Guardians was close to the Keeper. Mr Buckley had been with Mr Law and Jack was his companion, Emile Dupont must have one too.

"Where will we go first?" asked Tom.

"Nearest first sounds good to me." Jack studied the map closely.

The three excited adventurers packed their rucksacks with food, water and weapons. Felix and Tom had a whistle stop tour of a pistol and were told to use it only when really needed. Jack hid his sabre under his trench coat and they set off on their quest for Monsieur Emile Dupont.

12

Felix's father had been right. Paris was a beautiful old city. The sun beat down as they walked through the narrow, cobbled streets. The streets were coming to life; shops were opening and people were scurrying to work. The smell of freshly baked bread filled their nostrils. The only sign that France was at war was the odd pair of German soldiers walking together chatting peacefully about life back home. They would also catch sight of the German Nazi flag fluttering in the light summer breeze; its red background showing off what they knew was the most hated swastika symbol. The buildings were tall and made of old stone bricks; they were adorned with light coloured shutters that were bursting open as the inhabitants stirred. The street got wider and lighter as they approached its end. They found themselves opposite Notre Dame Cathedral on the banks of the River Seine. The river was teeming with boats taking goods and people back and forth. It was a hive of activity. Felix looked at the beautiful scene for a moment then took out his phone to take a photograph.

"What are you doing you fool?" whispered Jack.

"Taking a photo!" Felix thought it was a stupid question.

"That hasn't been invented yet!" Tom exclaimed, grabbing Felix's Mobile phone and throwing it in his pocket with his own.

"If the Germans or the conspirators see that they'll know we are spies and we'll be taken away like the rest," explained Jack.

"Sorry, I wasn't thinking," came Felix's apologetic reply.

They turned left and headed along the river towards the location of the nearest red sword on the map.

Felix and Tom behaved like tourists and could not help but look around at the scenery. The pair forgot about everything they were going through as they became immersed in the Paris scenes. Jack brought them back to reality when he pulled them up a very narrow alleyway.

"Not too far now. Be ready for anything." Jack was wary of the dangers of the Parisian back streets.

They weaved their way through the deserted back lanes. Tall buildings blocked out the sunlight, creating an eerie atmosphere. Felix was feeling scared as he didn't know what they would find. Jack stopped next to a red stable door and knocked hard. After a few minutes a flustered red faced French man opened the top half of the door.

"Oui!" he snarled angrily. Jack opened his coat to reveal his gleaming sabre. The door was opened and the trio were invited in. The door was slammed and locked tightly behind them.

"What now?" asked Tom, "This guy is strange."

"He's a Guardian, we'll be fine," reassured Felix.

Introductions were made; the Guardians name was Jean-Claude. He spoke good English and appeared pleased to see them.

"At last," he smiled, "The Keeper is here."

"Yes and No," replied Jack. "This is the Keeper but he has come from the future. We need to find the Keeper of 1944 to help this young man return home."

"I see." Jean-Claude scratched his head. "There are already three of us looking for the Keeper. We are close but we cannot find him; we think he is in hiding."

"Where?" Felix was desperate to learn how to travel forward in time.

"Somewhere here." Jean Claude pointed his finger to an area on Jack's map. "Somewhere between the three of us."

"Why haven't you found him?" asked Jack.

"That area is the centre of intensive German action at the moment," replied Jean-Claude, "we can't fight the Germans *and* the Brethren."

"Why are the Germans there?" asked Felix.

"Nobody knows, but it's too dangerous for us to go in there," replied their new friend.

"Well there's six of us now!" Tom piped up. "I really want to get home."

Jean-Claude looked pensive. He was silent for a few minutes, then smiled. "Let's do it, I'll get the others. Meet here at 9 tonight but be careful. It will be after the curfew."

During the German occupation there had been an 8pm curfew enforced on the Parisians to stop any undercover night time operations. The streets would be patrolled and if they were caught they would be sent to a prisoner of war camp or worse. They might be treated as spies and executed.

They decided to enjoy the Paris sunshine whilst they could and found a riverside café. Felix asked for a coffee to wake him up. Tom, always wanting to be the big man, asked the friendly waitress for an espresso and Jack ordered a beer. The drinks came quickly. The espresso came in a cup the size of a thimble and was so thick you could stand your spoon up in it. Jack laughed as Tom downed his drink in one gulp. Tom felt a surge of energy and his eyes opened wide.

"Next time ask for a coffee with milk," giggled Felix "Espressos will keep you awake all night - and you don't need extra energy!"

They meandered round the Paris markets, sampling the fresh fruit and taking in the fragrances of the flowers, meats and cheeses. They enjoyed being tourists for a few hours without a care in the world. The boys took lots of photographs holding their phones under their jackets. They got back to the safe house where Jack's friend was waiting. He looked sheepish.

"What's up Trev?" enquired Jack.

"We've been raided by the Gestapo, they looked everywhere," he replied angrily.

"What were they looking for?" Felix hoped he wouldn't answer, 'you.'

"Anything old they said, they took some paintings and pottery and left." Trevor shrugged his shoulders.

"Why?" asked Tom. "They starting an antiques shop?"

"Hitler has ordered the collection of antiques and old books and for them to be shipped to Berlin before Paris is liberated," explained Jack. "They wouldn't have found much here."

Felix and Tom had seen this in the film "Monument Men" the previous year. They had gone on a double date where Felix was too nervous to talk and Tom showed off so much the girls just left, never to be seen again. The film was about a group of antiques experts whose mission was to save artwork and antiques from the Germans. The boys had been lucky, being tourists had paid off. If they had been in the house they may have been captured.

"Lucky escape," said Jack laughing, "We have three hours until we are off."

Jack explained to Trevor they were going to rescue another operative from a safe house in an area swarming with Germans.

"Count me in." Trevor obviously missed the action of the front line. "I'll get what we need together, and you go and get some shut eye."

They slept through the afternoon. None of them knew what lay ahead that evening, but they knew it would not be dull.

13

Trevor woke the trio at 8 for dinner. For once it was not bread, cheese and ham. It was a fantastic chicken stew that would give them the energy to fulfil their mission. He had also prepared their weapons. He informed them that maps and papers were sown into the lining of their trousers just in case they got into any trouble.

Felix was filled with nerves. This was the first time he felt he was really putting himself in danger. He once again had a pistol but he did not know if he could use it.

"Cut it out!" Felix whispered to Tom as he rolled around the living room playing Cowboys and Indians, pretending to shoot anything that moved. Jack tried his best to lighten the mood with jokes and tales of daring do during his time in Northern France, but the nerves did not go. As he tucked The Book of Words into the waistband of his trousers, Felix wondered whether the Germans were all he had to worry about tonight. They covered their faces in boot polish, much to Tom's pleasure, to hide their faces in the moonlight. The group slipped quietly out of the back door leaving Trevor to await their return.

They crept quietly in the dark through the back alleys and lanes. Every now and again they hid from the beam of a patrol's torches. The patrols seemed amateur, taking cursory glances up and down the side streets as they walked along the main thoroughfares. It only took twenty minutes to reach Jean-Claude's house. The stable door was opened and they were greeted like long lost friends. Two shadowy figures lurked in the back room. Felix, Tom and Jack were introduced to Patrick and Leon, the other Guardians.

Patrick was short, only coming up to Jack's shoulders, but he made up for his lack of height with his muscle and bulk. He looked like a bulldog and looked like he would take no nonsense. Leon was the complete opposite; a tall, thin giant of a man. They both had beaming smiles and like everyone else were covered in boot polish.

"These guys look like they mean business." smiled Tom.

"For God sake just do as you're told, this isn't paintballing. We could die!" Felix trembled with fear.

The Guardians discussed their search pattern of the area. They also had an escape plan. They would split up and meet back at Trevor's safe house. The Germans had searched that area earlier so did not have any further interest there. They seemed confident that they would find Emile.

"Where is he?" asked Felix.

"We have narrowed it down to these three streets." Patrick pointed at his map.

"The Germans are everywhere there," announced Leon.

"What are our chances of getting him?" asked Tom, more worried about getting back home than anything else.

"We'll get back," grimaced Jean-Claude, "but your chances are slim."

Tom slumped into a chair as the others laughed out loud. Felix took out The Book of Words and asked if it knew where The Keeper was. The reply was confusing:

'You are The Keeper'

Felix looked at the map. Four red swords were in one place. He asked where Emile Dupont was. After what felt like an hour to Felix, but was actually less than a minute, the reply appeared:

'There is danger ahead and all around you. Beware the Brethren'

"The Book says to beware the Brethren," cried Felix, causing the others to become silent.

"Great," sighed Tom, "we're dead!"

Felix gave Tom one of his stern looks as he realised they were asking the others to put their lives in danger to protect him from the Brethren. 'We could just stay in 1944,' thought Felix, 'then nobody dies.' But he knew that wasn't an option.

The six odd looking warriors made their way out of the stable door and into the pitch black alleyway. There was little trouble as they approached the area in which they thought they would find Emile. The odd German search patrol was avoided through blending into the shadows and hiding behind walls. The Guardians looked concerned. Leon, who was the strongest character and the leader by default, pointed to a side building next to an empty restaurant and the group scurried in.

"Are your ears burning?" Leon asked the others

"Mine are freezing." Tom thought they were all going mad.

"Not you fool, the Guardians. It's how we sense the Keeper," snarled Patrick.

Felix and Tom looked at Jack quizzically.

"You know hide and seek? Warmer, colder?" whispered Jack.

"Of course," said Tom, rolling his eyes at Felix.

"Well it's a game that has come from the early training for Guardians. Our ears get warmer as we get closer to a Keeper," Jack explained.

"All our ears are burning at the moment, we know it's not Emile as he is too far away," said Patrick. "It must be you!" He pointed at Felix.

The four had a discussion and turned to Felix. "You will have to wait here. We'll find Emile and bring him to you." Felix accepted he was of no use to the Guardians and made himself comfortable in a smelly old armchair to await their return.

"I'll wait here too, keep him company," said Tom quietly.

"No chance my little cherub." Leon patted him on the back. "We need you for our plan."

Tom waved and mouthed something undecipherable in the dark to Felix and then the Guardians and Tom were gone.

14

Tom was petrified when the group of warriors left the shed. He didn't want to leave his best friend behind. He had always been there for Felix through thick and thin. He saw Felix as his equal but Tom knew that others dismissed his mate's lack of physical prowess as a weakness. Felix had been bullied since he had known him; but their friendship was forged when Tom had retrieved a tricycle from a big girl, who had pushed Felix off it and ridden off into the nursery garden, and given it back to Felix. Tom was proud of Felix as he was intelligent and could usually think his way through life. This little trip into the past was stretching both of them to the limit.

He followed the Guardians like a lost puppy, knowing that his only chance of getting through this was to do as he was told and stick to the Guardians like glue.

"Get your pistol out," whispered Jack.

Tom delved into his rucksack and pulled out the weapon. His hand shook so much he almost dropped it. Jack put his arm round him and said, "This is to get you home, just stick with me, point and shoot when I start shooting." Tom nodded. "And only shoot the bad men," added Jack with a huge grin on his face. Tom nodded, smiled, gripped the pistol firmly and followed Jack closely.

Leon led the shadowy figures through the back streets towards a brightly lit main road. Search lights shone down on the houses as groups of German soldiers entered noisily. The group crouched behind a parked lorry. Rows of German trucks lined the street. Soldiers were running everywhere, some ushering the scared inhabitants of the houses down towards the river while some loaded paintings and furniture onto trucks. The civilians clutched suitcases and bundles full of possessions and clothes.

"We have to get to stay low," whispered Leon, "down to the river."

"Are we swimming?" Tom asked Jack.

"Maybe, it depends on the river level," he replied.

The Guardians slinked over the road and down the embankment to the river's edge. They sidled along a narrow ledge past the German search lights. One by one they climbed back up to the road and quietly crossed into a narrow alley. The Germans were so busy they would not have noticed a herd of elephants marching down the street.

Their concentration was disturbed by an almighty explosion. The blast and smoke seemed to come from the near Jean-Claude's house. The Guardians looked at each other in a way that told Tom this meant trouble. The last time he had seen smoke this thick had been back at Queen Anne's School. He knew what would come next.

"Brethren?" he whispered to Patrick.

"Oui, mon ami," the stocky Patrick replied. "They are here. We have to get the Keeper and fast."

Tom turned to Jack and stated what they were all thinking, "But Felix is a Keeper too. What if they go for him?"

"I think your friend will be OK. If he is clever he will stay put until we return." Tom saw that Leon wasn't too convinced by his own statement.

Tom wanted to run back to Felix and tell him what was happening, to warn him about the Brethren. He soon accepted he was going to have to stay here, but if he had guessed the Brethren were here he was sure Felix would have too. Felix was bright. He would get back to Trevor if he had to.

Leon whispered, "Come on, vite, quickly." Once again the Guardians moved on.

They rounded the corner and entered the back yard of one of the houses. Leon opened the door, scratching his ears hard. The Guardians sensed Emile was close. They searched the house, they even sent Tom up in to the dark, dusty attic to search. Emile was nowhere to be found. They sat in the kitchen planning their next move. Tom suddenly jumped up and grabbed a jug of water.

"What the hell are you doing?" To Jack's surprise Tom began pouring water all over the kitchen tiles.

"The Great Escape!" squealed Tom, "Great film! This is how they found the tunnel."

"The Great what?" Jack had never heard that phrase before.

Tom laughed as he realised that the film wasn't going to be made for twenty years. "It's a film. The Germans pour coffee on tiles and the coffee trickled through when it dropped into a tunnel."

"Genius!" Leon grabbed a vase and emptying the contents onto the floor. He smiled as he heard a trickling. He unpicked a broken tile to find a metal hook. They pulled on the improvised handle and there huddled together in a small burrow were three figures: a woman, a teenage boy and a toddler.

"Emile?" asked Leon.

"Oui!" cried the boy, as he sprung up holding a bejewelled broad sword above his head ready to attack. Emile was a couple of years older than Felix and Tom but a lot taller and stockier, his curly black hair bobbed up and down as he jumped out of the hiding hole.

"We're Guardians!" exclaimed Patrick before Emile had a chance to strike.

A look of relief spread across Emile's face as he called for his mother and brother to join him amongst friends. The little boy was bawling uncontrollably. Leon quickly explained why they had come and that the Brethren weren't far away. As they prepared to move they heard a voice that sent a shiver down all their spines, "The Keeper, Emile Dupont. Where are you?"

Tom knew what was about to appear and stood behind Jack. The Guardians drew their sabres, four gleaming blades, one for each of the Brethren monks. Emile stood with them ready for the fight, his mother and brother joined Tom behind the awaiting warriors.

"What about Felix?" screamed Tom.

"He's right, we need to get Emile to Felix." Jack knew it was the only chance of getting Felix and Tom home.

Leon nodded in agreement. Jean-Claude clasped Leon's shoulder. "I will stay with you!"

Leon smiled and ordered Jack and Patrick to take the Duponts and Tom to safety. Without hesitation Jack pushed the family through the front door of the house and onto the main street. Tom waved to Leon and followed. He looked back as he heard the back door crash in and Leon and Jean-Claude charged at the Brethren.

The Germans were still busy searching and looting the houses down the street and were oblivious to the escapees running across the street to the river.

"We've only got one chance of getting to Trevor's house." said Jack. "We have to cross the river to avoid the German search. We can double back at the next bridge."

Patrick disappeared along the river bank and returned moments later with a small rowing boat which was only big enough for four. Jack smirked at Tom and loaded the Dupont family into the boat.

"Come on," he barked at Tom as he finished loading the Duponts into the boat. Tom assumed he was about to get wet, and he was right. He slowly lowered himself into the freezing waters of the Seine. Any breath Tom had left his body in an almighty gasp as he submerged.

"No splashing," smiled Jack as he pushed off across the river. Tom reluctantly followed. The pair reached the opposite bank, tired, cold and soaked through. They ran to meet Patrick upstream, the strong current had carried them some distance away from the boat as they swam.

They re-joined Patrick and the Duponts and crept quickly along the river bank. Tom was shivering now but he knew he could not feel sorry for himself, he had to get to Felix. In no time they were approaching the bridge which would lead them back to Felix, and to Trevor's house. Patrick pointed across to a group of German soldiers dragging a prisoner along the road on the opposite side of the river. The shadowy figure looked familiar.

15

Every five minutes the beams of searching flashlights flickered through the shed window. Felix was sitting in the middle of a German search. He wondered if they were aware of his presence and their search was for him. He did not feel safe and decided that he had to move, but he didn't know when it would be safe.

The choice was made for him as the shed was shaken by an almighty blast. There were no bombings in Paris during the war, the odd resistance action, but nothing like this. His body stiffened, his mind froze. He had seen this thick smoke that crept through the air before. It was the Brethren! They were here. They were after the Book. He peeked through a gap in the shed walls as four ghostly figures strode past. It was the monks!

Felix waited a few minutes and left the shed. He crawled across the courtyard of the restaurant and onto the street. Staying close to the buildings he worked his way slowly away from the monsters. At a junction he could hear voices and breaking wood. He peered round the building and saw hundreds of soldiers pulling people onto the street and marching them down towards the river. The contents of the houses were being thrown through windows onto the street where they splintered into firewood. Another group were loading pictures, antique furniture and old books into trucks that sped away, once filled, towards the railway yard.

He heard a voice that sent a shiver down his spine.

"The Keeper, Emile Dupont. Where are you?" came the gravelly call.

He cowered in a dark doorway behind a large cart. The monks floated past onto the main road and headed towards the chaos. The Germans seemed to take the appearance of the monks in their stride. The German Captain spoke to the Brethren and they disappeared into a building. There were clashes of steel, the Guardians inside were putting up a fight. He was alone; the Guardians would die and he would never get back to London and home. He felt a momentary despair. He opened the Book and whispered, "What now?"

Follow your instinct, follow their instructions

Felix's instinct was to run. Their instructions were to meet at Trevor's. He was getting good at running but he was lost. He looked at the Book but it was too faint to read in the growing darkness. He looked at the map but wasn't sure he could follow it accurately through the night-time streets. He decided that if he got to the river he could remember his way back. The clashing blades filled the air ahead, the Guardians were a lot younger than Mr Buckley and the battle seemed ferocious. Felix had to get back to the safety of Trevor's house.

Felix stumbled out onto the road next to the river. It was doused in moonlight and compared to the back lanes it was like walking in daylight. He could see the patrols and would quickly dart into a dark doorway or behind a wall to evade them. He started to recognise the landscape. On the far side of the river he could see six strange figures keeping low and heading in the same direction as him. He looked carefully at them. It was Jack, Patrick and Tom, accompanied by three smaller figures he assumed were Emile and his family. His mood lightened, he would soon be safe with his friends and on his way home.

He was close now. Two more side streets and he would turn off the dangerous main road. A patrol appeared in the distance, so he darted up an alley. He crouched behind a bin and waited for the inevitable flash of light before he could continue his journey. The flash came, he waited a minute and stood up.

"Halt," came the call.

He turned to run but he was surrounded. Two soldiers had been having a cigarette at the top of the alley and had seen him crouch down. The patrol had heard the cry and had the exit blocked. He reached into his pocket for the pistol but realised his chance of survival would be slim. He gave himself up and went quietly. He whistled defiantly as he was dragged along the river bank. Felix looked desperately at the group on the far bank. The tune he made was "It's a long way to Tipperary". Jack must have recognised the tune as he waved and gave him the thumbs up. He knew they would try and rescue him.

16

It was a short march. Felix squirmed to make the book fall into the backside of his trousers. He was slung roughly into a large, noisy wooden warehouse. The building was packed with people of all ages. Some were crying, some singing and a few praying, but most just stood in shock. A small group of children sat in a circle playing some sort of game. Felix slowly walked over. They invited him to join them in their game. He immediately turned to the girl next to him and asked, "Why are we all here?"

"Mother says we are being taken to a camp to work for the Germans," she replied.

"No, my dad said we are going to see my uncle and his family who left last year. We haven't seen them since." chirped a happy looking teenager.

"My grandparents said we're going on an adventure," said a sick pasty looking boy.

The truth hit Felix like a brick in the face. He had been rounded up with a group of French Jews. Having studied this period of time in History with Mr Taylor he knew exactly what was happening. He, like them, would be shipped by train or boat to a death camp in the East of the German's territory. The horror was too much to bear. He would never get out of this one. Felix began sobbing uncontrollably.

He had come all this way and was about to make his last journey. He retired to a dark and quiet corner of the room.

"What about Tom?" he muttered quietly to himself. Felix wondered if his best friend and true guardian would make it home in one piece. He looked at the unknowing crowd before him, then opened the Book and asked "How do I get out of this one clever clogs?"

'I will see you right.'

'A great reply,' thought Felix. His lifesaver was now this tatty old book. If only he knew how he had got here then he could use the Book in the same way to get home.

A German voice made an announcement over a loud but crackly public announcement system. The crowd were told to make their way towards the open door at the far end of their prison. Felix was near the back of the tense throng. He could see some people being searched and their personal possessions and money being confiscated and placed in containers. Some managed to squeeze past with everything they could carry. The queue of people was ushered into the next warehouse for the next stage of their humiliation. The guards were sure to find the Book. Felix had no choice but to do as he was told; there was nowhere to run.

The end of a rifle pressed against his back as Felix was pushed towards a searching table. The waiting soldier looked quizzically at Felix's watch and slipped it into his pocket. Felix had seen searches at football matches; he knew they would now pat him down, searching all over his body. It took them seconds to find The Book of Words. As the soldier was about to throw it in a wooden box a cane was thrust across his chest. A formidable blonde man looked Felix up and down. His uniform was black, different to the others. There were skull badges on his hat and shoulders, this was the Gestapo. The officer grabbed the Book and led Felix away with his other hand. He was taken to a small office area which was full of worried looking administrators taking phone calls and filing papers. They were obviously getting news of the invasion and the retreat of the German army. The Gestapo officer grabbed a phone and made an animated call. His smile told Felix all he needed to know. He was going somewhere he did not want to go.

Felix's hands were tied and he was bundled into the back of a jeep. A soldier sat on each side of him, and the Gestapo officer jumped on to the passenger seat. The journey was short and it was only ten minutes before he was thrown from the back of the jeep. Felix was marched across a yard filled with crates and into a building. They smacked his head every time he tried to look up so he stared at the floor.

"Is the Book yours?" shouted his inquisitor.

Felix looked up defiantly into the Nazi's icy blue eye [there was a patch over the other] and replied, "So what if it is?"

"Is it yours?" he was asked again, as the Gestapo officer twisted his bindings so they burnt his arms.

"What use is an old book to you?" asked Felix.

"Is it yours?" his captor asked again, as a pistol was cocked and placed against his head. Thinking quickly, Felix realised that the Book was useless without him. There was no way the Germans would shoot him if they knew about The Book of Words. It was a chance he could afford to take.

"Never seen it before." Felix decided to deny everything.

"Your cheek will get you nowhere. Lock him up. We'll continue this in Berlin." The officer was visibly angry and he had lost all patience with Felix.

The Book had saved him. A million questions whizzed round his mind. He didn't know why the Germans wanted the Book. He wondered how much they knew about The Book of Words. He'd been to Berlin on a school trip, he was sure it would be different this time. Felix was terrified, he knew what the Nazis were capable of. He was scared of what would greet him in the German capital. He had to get the Book back and keep it safe. The Book was his responsibility now. This was his first and only job and right now he was failing dismally. He was afraid he would be another nameless victim of Hitler's regime. His prison was cold and damp; there was no furniture and it was dark. He banged on the walls but they were concrete - no way out through them. His guard gave him bread and water regularly but he did not say much. All Felix could do was await his fate.

17

Tom, exhausted, freezing cold and scared to death, stumbled into Trevor's kitchen followed by Emile, his startled family and Patrick. Trevor, who had been waiting impatiently for their return, sprang to his feet and collected blankets from the large pirate chest near the stove. Tom helped Emile wrap up his mother and younger brother in front of the roaring fire in the living room.

"Where's Jack?" asked Trevor.

"Following Felix, I hope!" replied a shivering Tom as he huddled by the stove for warmth.

"The Nazis have Felix. Jack's gone to rescue him," added Patrick as he washed the boot polish from his face.

"On his own?" shrieked Trevor, worried for his friend. "I'm going after him."

"No!" ordered a stern Patrick, "This is a one man job."

Tom added, "Felix will be OK. With the Book he can speak German. He'll talk his way out of it like he always does!" He hoped that he was right and Felix would survive his ordeal. Trevor had prepared food and they all tucked into a steaming casserole.

Emile, recovered from his rescue, asked "Why is Felix so important?"

Tom walked angrily towards Emile shouting. "He's my best mate to start with, and he is The Keeper."

Emile calmly said, "He will be fine, the Book will see him safe."

"I hope so," said Tom, "the only problem is he doesn't know how to use it!"

Emile's expression changed, "What do you mean?" Tom told the tale of how they had got to Paris.

64

"Has he got the Keeper's sword?" asked Emile.

"He didn't have it when we left school," replied Tom, "we don't know how we got here."

"He doesn't know how to travel?" Emile looked worried.

"No, that's why we need you to tell us how to get home," shouted Tom, agitated by the French boy's persistent questions.

A breathless Jack burst through the back door into the kitchen.

"Where the hell is Felix?" shouted Tom.

"He's at the railway yard, there's no way of getting him. There are Germans everywhere." said a tearful Jack. "I've failed as a Guardian."

"Not yet you haven't." Emile said with a big grin, "Where are they taking him?"

"Berlin." Jack was beside himself with worry.

"The Guardians will find him. He'll be fine." Patrick stated without much confidence.

"At least he's seeing the world," laughed Tom hysterically.

"I'll go to Berlin and get him in the morning," winked Emile. "All I need is a photograph of Berlin from today. They obviously know about the Book or he would be in the sheds with the others. They won't touch him if they think he is The Keeper."

"Just one question," added Emile, "how long have you been in 1944?"

"Too long!" quipped an exhausted Tom.

"They've been here five days" said Jack helpfully, looking daggers at Tom. His humour was wearing thin.

"We only have two days to get him back," Emile whispered, "More than 7 days and you will disappear from this time and yours, forgotten for ever." He became thoughtful, "Any more questions?" he asked.

"What are you still doing here?" Tom chortled.

They all fell about laughing knowing nothing more could be done until the morning.

Tom was the first awake and ran down to the news stand to buy all the day's papers. He got back and tore through each one. "Where are you?" he screamed at the messy pile of paper in front of him, "Give me just one picture of Berlin."

Emile appeared yawning and smiling at Tom. He walked straight over and picked up a picture of Hitler saluting an expectant crowd.

"This will do," he said pointing at the snap.

"How do you travel?" asked Tom.

"I just hold the Book and jump into the picture," smiled Emile. "I'll wake up somewhere in that square," he added.

"Right!" said Tom, thinking hard until the penny dropped. "We fell against the wall - a poster of the D day invasion. So all we have to do is find a picture of where we came from and jump in."

"Not quite, where is there a picture of the future in 1944?" shrugged Emile.

With that Emile picked up his sword, laid the paper on the floor and jumped. Tom rugby tackled him across the kitchen, crashing into the crockery cupboard.

"What did you do that for?" screamed Emile.

Tom smiled. "How will you get back here?"

Emile laughed and patted Tom on the back. "Good thinking, we'll make a Guardian out of you yet," he whispered to Tom.

Tom had a brainwave. He took out his phone, took a snap of the kitchen and then showed Emile how to get the picture back on the screen. Wide mouthed and shocked at his new toy, Emile smiled and jumped into the photograph of Berlin. He was gone.

18

Before his eyes could adjust to the bright sunlight that burst through his prison cell door, Felix was picked up and carried through the air. As he was dragged across the freight yard he saw lots of antiques being loaded into carriages. The blonde Gestapo officer pointed to a small wooden crate next to the large steam engine which Felix assumed was his seat for the journey to Berlin. The crate was brought to the officer. At first, Felix had the horrible thought that *he* would be squeezed inside the tiny crate for the long journey to Berlin, but sighed with relief as the crate was filled with hay and the book placed safely in the middle. The crate was loaded into the officer's carriage at the back of the train. Felix was made to follow it. He was locked in a small bedroom; at least he would be comfortable on this trip. He lay back and wondered how he would get out of this one.

Felix prayed there would be a Guardian, or even better, an army of them in Berlin waiting to rescue him and The Book of Words. From his knowledge of Europe he knew the journey would take some time, so he lay back on his small bunk and relaxed. The room was comfortable; he had a bed, a sink and a window. At least he could watch the world fly by whilst he summoned all his wits to think about how he could get the book back. He had seen films where the hero had climbed onto the roof of a train, had a death defying fight rolling around on each carriage and then saved the world. He was no James Bond. He chuckled to himself as his ideas became more and more absurd. He would have to sit and wait until he got to Berlin.

He sat at the small desk under the window and leaned on his hands. The countryside flashed in front of his eyes: trees, flower filled fields, small picturesque villages, hordes of German troops heading north to support the failing defensive lines. This part of France had escaped the ravages of war and was beautiful. He reached into his pocket for his phone to take some photos. It was gone. He remembered Tom had taken it the day before. His mind's internal camera was turned on. He must remember what the region looked like so he could visit it in the future to see if it was the same. Eventually, bored and tired, he lay on the bed and drifted off to sleep.

He dreamt of home and his normal life. He played football with his mates and walked home afterwards with his best friend Tom. He played merrily on his game console and went to school. Then the Brethren appeared and chased him round the school with their swords. Mr Buckley battled with them but could not keep them away. Just as the monks were about to bury their swords into Felix he woke up, wet through with sweat.

He splashed water on his face to wake himself up. Felix thought of Tom, wondering if he was safe with Jack. He laughed as he thought about Tom probably being a pain in the neck. A knock on the door brought food and water. 'Even the Germans are at it!' he laughed, as he scoffed down bread, ham and cheese. The train slowed and came to a halt. He could hear the hustle and bustle of a busy city outside. He lifted the blind and could not believe his eyes. They had stopped for water in a hellhole. Hardly a building stood without damage. People rushed about their normal business between piles of rubble. Older soldiers, too old for fighting at the front, guided operations around the station. The officer came into the room and pulled the blind down.

"You shouldn't see this," he said.

"Why not? You're losing the war and Berlin will fall by the summer," said Felix through a smirk.

He laughed. "Never! We are regrouping and mounting a counter offensive as we speak."

"We'll see," murmured Felix. "How much further to Berlin?"

"A couple of hours. Keep the blind shut." The officer ordered. "You're going somewhere very special when we get there."

Felix lay back on the bed and contemplated what he would encounter in Berlin.

19

Felix jumped up as the train juddered and began to slow down. Although he was scared to death, Felix pulled himself to his full height and told himself he was The Keeper. The Book was useless without him and he was not going to be intimidated. The train came to a full stop and he heard the officer's boots stomp up the corridor to his room. The door opened and the officer greeted him with a smile.

"I am the luckiest officer in the Gestapo," he said with a wink, "and you are the luckiest Jewish boy in Paris."

"I'm not..." Felix stopped as he thought. "They think I'm Emile," he whispered quietly.

That's why they were searching there – the Jewish quarter. Somehow they all knew the Keeper was Jewish. He would play along for now, but he hated the thought of what would happen if they found out.

Felix smiled at the officer and followed him off the train. There waiting for them was a bright shiny car with flags on its bonnet, filled with people in uniforms covered in medals and stripes. They were obviously important. An empty car sat behind them and a car filled with soldiers came next. The wooden crate was placed in the first car, much to the delight of the big wigs within. Felix was bundled into the second car where the Gestapo officer joined him on the back seat. The convoy left the station and picked its way through the bombed out industrial sector of Berlin.

Lines of people cleared rubble from what used to be their homes. Small fires consumed what was left of buildings. The war was hitting Germany hard. Felix knew it was a matter of months before the British, Americans and Russians would divide the city up and life here would change forever. His wry smile brought a slap around the head.

"What do you find so funny about this?" asked the officer.

"Nothing, it's sad, but I know what's coming."

"Silence!" screamed the officer.

They drove for thirty minutes into an area where the buildings were more ornate and the smell of the fires drifted on the air. Felix was marched up some steep stone steps towards a huge black metal door. The building had been protected from the bombing so it must be important. Scared and trembling, Felix was led down a long corridor with old paintings and sculptures lining the walls. It smelled of polish - the dark wooden floor was gleaming. At the end of the corridor Felix was ushered into a small office where two soldiers pointed their rifles at him, ensuring that all thoughts of escape rapidly disappeared.

Two ladies appeared in nurses' uniforms. They were smiling and made Felix feel at ease. One reminded him of his grandmother with her grey hair tied up in a bun. The other filled a bowl with warm water and began washing his face with a flannel. He hadn't bathed for days and must have looked a sight. He was brought new clothes and shiny, black shoes. He wondered what he was being prepared for. He knew whoever he was about to meet was important to these people, but he knew that *he* was also important to them. Next came a hot meal, and this time it was served on a large white porcelain plate. The beef roast dinner was delicious. It was the first good meal Felix had eaten since getting to France. He did ask himself if this was the last meal of a condemned boy.

Following the meal he was asked to stand up and the nurses straightened his clothes. This was it. Felix was about to be reunited with The Book of Words. He left the office and found the Gestapo officer waiting outside an oak door.

20

"Ready?" the beaming officer enquired.

"As I'll ever be," replied Felix.

The officer knocked twice on the door. Another officer opened the door and saluted with the usual straight arm. After a returned salute Felix was marched in. The room was huge, the size of the whole of the downstairs of Felix's home back in England. The walls were filled with masterpieces. The officer walked Felix through the throng of German Generals to a table. The large board room table was covered in maps including one whose paper looked familiar. Next to it sat the book.

A side door squeaked open. In walked a face Felix recognised. He gulped as the whole room stood to attention and saluted. It was Adolf Hitler.

Hitler greeted Felix like a long lost friend. In perfect German Felix asked "What do you want with me?"

"You are who we are looking for. You are the Keeper," replied the German leader.

Felix realised his suddenly acquired language skills had given him away. The Book was working its magic.

"What do you want with me?" Felix repeated.

"You will turn the tide of this war," laughed Hitler, pointing at the Book and the adjacent map.

Felix realised the map was the missing second page of the Book. Again there were only questions running round in his head, none of which he had answers for.

"How can I win a war on my own?" he squeaked nervously.

"You can open the Book and its secrets," snarled Hitler.

"I don't know what you mean," Felix responded.

"When this map is replaced the Book's full power will be restored. We have been waiting a very long time for this moment. The map shows us where our enemies are and where they are weakest; but with the Book we will be able to know what they are going to do before they do." he cackled. "You will ensure that by becoming our agent."

Felix knew he would be able to travel through time and see what plans were being made by the allies, but he did not know *how* to travel. Anyway, he would not allow this tyrant to rule the whole world.

"The book will give you information that will let us overpower any army who dares to oppose us," added Hitler.

"I won't do it!" screamed Felix.

"You will have little choice. We have ways of making you talk." laughed The Fuhrer. A man in a white doctor's coat appeared holding a large needle. 'Truth drugs!' thought Felix. They may be able to control him after all.

The side door opened once more and Felix felt his heart stop. In strode four creatures - half human, half skeleton - dressed in monks' cloaks. They drew their blood soaked swords and walked towards him laughing demonically. The Germans were working with the Brethren! He had to think and act quickly.

"Give me the Book," said Felix in a defeated way. Hitler slid it across the table. Felix opened it and asked "What do I do now?"

The page remained blank, "It's not working!" he shouted at Hitler.

"Make it work!" Hitler bellowed.

"I can't!" Felix screamed back. He looked at the map on the first page. What he saw amazed him and he immediately felt a little safer. The Brethren moved closer. To halt them he picked the Book up and flicked through the pages. Hitler ordered all of the Generals to leave. The Gestapo officer was ordered to stay as he had found the Book and the Keeper.

Hitler was visibly angry. His face was beetroot red and his wide open eyes stared straight at Felix. He strode purposefully over to Felix and raised his hand high above his head. Felix shut his eyes waiting for the blow to rain down on his head. There was a thud but no pain.

21

He opened his eyes and couldn't believe what he saw. A marching stick had blocked Hitler's arm. The Gestapo officer had come to his rescue. Hitler reeled backwards in a state of confusion; one of his own had dared to strike him!

The officer winked again at Felix and from his stick drew a hidden sabre. The map had been right! The red flashing symbol had shown that there was a Guardian in the building. Hitler ran towards them. The Brethren went into attack mode. The officer grabbed Felix and dragged him under the table.

"This is my destiny," he whispered excitedly. "The greater cause of a free world is better than dying for him."

"Have you your sword?" he asked.

"No," said Felix

"You take Mein Fuhrer with this, and I'll take the Brethren." He passed Felix his stick.

They jumped out to continue the fight. The Guardian fought ferociously, repelling each of the monks' blows. Sparks from the blades filled the room. Hitler chased Felix around the table. Felix turned and foolishly threw the stick at him. He dropped the Book in the chaos as he dodged swords and bodies as the Guardian deftly kept the Brethren at bay. Hitler picked up his great prize. Felix knew he had to get the book back and stopped running. Hitler dived at Felix. Felix reached out and grabbed at the German's face. The result sent him cowering into a corner. Felix had torn away half a mask revealing a skull. Hitler was one of the Brethren!

"Why?" asked Felix "Why kill so many just to get a tatty old book?"

"We knew the Keeper was likely to be Jewish," Hitler replied. "Germany was ready for a revolution, we just used it to our advantage."

Felix became angry; so many had died so they could get the Book. Hitler replaced his mask and drew a sword. The battle behind them seemed irrelevant as this all sank in to Felix's increasingly addled mind. He had no weapon, but at least he would be killed by someone famous.

There was a loud crash and the battle came to a sudden halt. The outside door had swung open and in burst a teenager looking a little bedraggled, but carrying a huge bejewelled silver sword. He had a Book tucked into his belt. Everyone looked with curiosity at this strange sight. Hitler screamed, "Another Keeper!"

'That must be Emile,' deduced Felix. The second Keeper threw the sword to Felix and cried, "I cannot use it now! Keep them occupied while I prepare our escape."

Felix remembered immediately the fencing lessons with Jack in the French fields on their journey to Paris. He worked his way towards the Guardian and as a double act they fended off the five attackers. Felix tired quickly, not being used to real battles, but he fought bravely remembering to defend until the opportunity came to attack. It didn't seem as if he would get the chance as the blows from The Brethren were relentless.

"Get the Book!" screamed Emile over the noise of battle.

"Go," said the Guardian. "I will keep them away."

Felix ran to the table and grabbed the Book from a startled Hitler's grasp. As Felix turned away he saw something quite strange. Emile was fiddling with a mobile phone - it was Felix's! Emile threw it on the floor and grabbed Felix's arm. They looked across the room to see the Brethren stepping over the Guardian's lifeless body and charging towards them.

"Jump!" shouted Emile.

The pair jumped onto the phone. As a hole opened in the floor they heard Hitler scream

"Noooooooooooooo".

Emile reached up through the hole and grabbed the phone just before the pair blacked out.

22

Felix awoke to a familiar sight. Flashing swirling spirals of colour intermingled with images of history. To his left was Emile wearing a huge smile. The French boy was dressed in a filthy white shirt and ripped grey trousers. Felix was safe but still had no real idea of what was happening. Emile had chosen to come to Berlin to rescue him, and a German who was his enemy was actually a Guardian. He was totally confused. Felix tried to figure it out. He attempted to speak but the whistling wind drowned out any sound he made. He struggled with the strange puzzle until he blacked out again.

When Felix woke again he was comfortable. This was very different to last time with the bombs. He wondered whether it had all been a dream and he had woken up in his own bed. The jolly "Come on old chap, up we get!" told him he was back in Paris with Jack. "Breakfast is ready."

Wearily Felix entered the kitchen. Emile was sat laughing with Tom and Trevor at the table, telling them of the events in Berlin.

Tom jumped up with glee when he saw his best friend. He gave him a huge hug that told Felix he had been scared and was so glad to see him again.

"You smacked Hitler?" laughed Tom. "You couldn't punch your way out of a paper bag and you take on the biggest nutter the world has known!"

Felix shrugged smugly and sat down for breakfast. On the table sat the usual bread, ham and cheese alongside two copies of The Book of Words. One had Felix's name emblazoned on the cover, the other had no name.

"What's happened to your book?" Felix asked Emile.

"Only one of the Books can be active if there are more than one of them in the same time and place. That honour falls to the Keeper from the future most date," replied Emile. "My book is useless until you have gone."

"I am Emile," he declared, realising they hadn't been introduced, "and you must be Felix." The pair shook hands, smiled at each other and sat down to eat. Jack and Trevor sat in the sitting room plotting and planning their next mission against the Germans.

"Thank you!" Felix said gratefully to Emile

"No need for thanks. You would have done the same," he replied.

"I have a burning question - how do we use the Book to travel?" asked Felix.

Tom laughed, "Haven't you worked that out yet?" He winked at Emile.

"How did you get here?" asked Emile grinning.

"We were running from the Brethren and they cornered us. I charged them and bounced into Tom and the wall. The next thing I knew we were in Normandy in 1944."

"What was the last thing you saw at home?" asked Tom giggling.

"Those ugly skeleton faced idiots," replied Felix.

"What was on the wall of the room?" asked a knowing Emile.

"A picture from the second world war. A view of the allied armada sailing towards...," he stopped talking. The lightbulb in his brain switched on. The book would transport you to the place and time shown in the picture you fell into!

"So if we can travel through pictures, how did we get back here from Berlin?"

"It was Tom's idea. I had to tell him our secret of travel. He had your communication device which also takes a photograph.

We took a photograph of the room and I found a picture in a newspaper of Hitler in Berlin from the day before. The rest, as we say, is History. I worked my way to the building following the red sword on the map there was only one and I knew Guardians head towards Keepers so I guessed you'd be there. Once I got close to you, my book became blank. Blind luck I suppose."

"So all I have to do is find pictures of places and dive right in?" asked Felix.

"Don't you know anything?" said Tom mocking Felix's lack of knowledge.

"Yep," smirked Emile. "It's handy when the Brethren come. They travel in a similar way but I've only ever seen four of them in one place until today."

"Why are they chasing down the Book?" queried Felix.

"I don't really know," said Emile. "I've only been a Keeper a few years and some of the powers are still a mystery to me."

Tom was beaming at being reunited with Felix. He sat patiently waiting for him to ask the obvious question.

"How can I get home? I have no pictures of today at home and I don't want to live in the past," said a worried Felix as he thought of his desperate parents searching for him.

"If there are no images then you must look in the place marked on the map for an object that is out of place. If you use that object you will return to where you came from. The memory of all that happened will be wiped from all those who witnessed it; and the Guardians and Keepers that died will be gone but not forgotten." added Emile. "You'll figure..."

"We know!" interrupted Tom, "Figure it out as we go." The three young boys laughed and pushed each other around the table.

"A bit confusing," said Felix scratching his head "but I think I get it."

81

Their conversation was cut short by Jack. He wanted to return Emile to his family, who were in hiding at a new safe house further up the river. Emile wished Felix and Tom well and disappeared into the bustling Paris crowds.

23

The boys were eager to get home but they had promised Jack that they would wait to see him before returning home. The pair chatted with Trevor about life in the future and some of the changes he would see. They didn't want to spoil too much for him though. Trevor told him of his ambition to be a schoolmaster on his return to England when the war was over. An hour of idle chit chat went by before Jack came bumbling through the door carrying a French stick of bread, "Emile is safe. Now let's get you home."

Felix opened the Book to the map. Nothing new appeared. His jaw dropped, the second page was missing. The Brethren still had it. It must have fallen out in Hitler's office.

"The map! It's gone!" he shrieked.

"What map?" asked Tom.

"Page two is a world map! The Brethren have it," Felix replied, knowing that the Brethren would continue their quest for the Book. His feeling of being safe evaporated. From now on every explosion could mean that they had come to take him back to their leader. Hitler was their leader now but he could not have always been. His brain was a muddled mess. He had to find out the full story about the Book. It had taken over his life and he knew nothing of it. None of The Keepers in the Book had lasted more than five years except one - The Sheriff. He must know more than anyone else. Felix would go back one day and interrogate him! For now he had to get back to the twenty first century. He did not care where. He figured he could find his way to England from anywhere in the world. He just wanted to go home and away from all of this.

Terrified about what they would face when they got home, he realised this danger would never disappear as long as the Brethren wanted the Book. He had a new duty and he vowed from this moment that whatever happened he would do as he had been asked, and keep the book safe. On telling Tom, his friend couldn't help himself, "Who the hell do you think you are? Superman!"

Felix gave him a withering look. His mind returning to their current plight. He was angry that the map had been lost. It had been back in the Book and he had let it slip from his grasp. It was obvious that if the map and Book were kept apart no great harm would come to the world. As long as he had the Book he would be in danger. It was a price he would have to pay.

Felix looked at Jack and repeated apologetically "They still have the map."

"But you have the book and the Guardians," Jack laughed as he waved his sabre in the air.

"And me," added Tom.

Felix smiled and nodded. He opened the book again. There in the middle of the map was a clock with the future date written on it, and the time showing ten o'clock. He did not have a clue what this meant. After much discussion they decided that it must mean that he had to be at that point at ten o'clock to find the way home. Trevor piped up, "It's quarter to now." In a massive panic they grabbed their school uniforms, put them in a rucksack and ran towards the place marked on the map - Notre Dame Cathedral.

24

As they reached the Latin Quarter, on the opposite bank of the Seine to the famous old landmark, Trevor checked his watch, "Five minutes to ten," he reported. They ran across the bridge and into the cathedral. They had two minutes to find whatever did not fit in that time. Notre Dame was huge. Felix and Tom looked at the fantastic stained glass windows and their rainbow of twinkling light that dazzled the eyes of the visitors and worshippers.

"Split up," said Jack. "Holler if you see anything"

"Old or new?" asked Trevor.

"There's plenty of old here, won't stick out much. Look for something that would fit in the future," Jack shouted as they ran in different directions.

They set off to different parts of the cathedral. There was an army of statues from medieval times, plenty of tapestries and paintings but nothing that stuck out as being new. A clock outside started to sound the ten o'clock chimes. They looked hurriedly under pews, in the pulpits, and high up in the vaulted ceiling amongst the huge wooden beams and carvings. The chimes stopped. They were too late.

"What now?" asked a gloomy Tom. Felix reached into his waist band and pulled out the Book. He opened it up to the map and it still showed the clock and date. He asked, "Where is the exit?"

'Ten o'clock comes twice a day ;-)'

"What's with the wink?" Felix giggled.

'Just down with the kids ☺'

85

"We'll have to come back tonight." Felix was pleased that they had another chance.

They had twelve hours to wait. They decided to visit Emile. Emile welcomed them in with open arms. His mother prepared a buffet lunch of food fresh from the market. The smells in the tiny kitchen were amazing: spiced meat, French cheese and fresh bread. It was obvious to them all that Emile's mother did not have a clue about the Book, the Guardians or the Brethren. It was a relaxing afternoon, which they all needed. They sat in the sun in the back yard and talked of life after the war. Jack looked as his watch and was shocked, as it showed that it was time to go before the Parisian curfew kicked in.

They made their way back to Trevor's house. At nine thirty they put on the compulsory boot polish and slinked through the backstreets to the Latin Quarter. They had hit their first obstacle - the German night guards on each bridge. They thought about swimming but the current was too strong.

"We need a diversion," said Trevor. "Will you three be able to manage on your own?"

"We'll be fine." Jack shook his friend's hand.

Trevor disappeared up the dark, narrow alley behind them. They sat under the bridge wondering what the diversion would be. They did not have to wait too long. The sky was filled with flames as an empty factory ignited in a matter of seconds. The accompanying explosion attracted the attention of every German within a mile. The guards on the bridge rushed past Jack and the boys, obviously thinking they may catch the resistance operating in this area.

The camouflaged trio kept low under the wall that ran the length of the bridge. They looked down to their left. There were boats being filled with people carrying suitcases and

86

bundles of belongings. A line of Jewish Parisians were walking out from a tunnel beneath the cathedral and being herded like cattle onto the awaiting boats. Felix stopped and sighed as he knew where the Jews were going to end up, and that very few of them would survive the war.

Jack grabbed Felix and hurried him along. A truck sped past them and headed down the ramp towards the boats. The tailgates opened and more people were bundled out of it and into the crowd. A lady screamed, "Jack!" The trio stopped and hid behind a pillar. They glanced at the lady - it was Emile's mother. Emile stood by her side carrying his younger brother and their bags. They were about to be shipped east.

"We have to get them," whispered Felix.

"We can't, we have to get you home. I'll come back once you're gone. I'll keep him safe - it *is* my job!"

Reluctantly Felix followed Jack and Tom to a back entrance to the cathedral. They had longer this time to search thoroughly for the exit point. Nothing stood out. There was nothing in the main body of the church. They entered the vestry and chambers to the side of the altar. Then they heard something they'd thought would not bother them again so soon.

"The Keeper, Felix Jones, where are you?" growled the gravelly voiced monster.

"The Brethren!" Felix and Tom said together. Jack drew his sword whilst the boys continued their search. Paintings, shelves full of trinkets and cupboards full of cassocks.

"Where the hell is it?" screamed Tom.

"Keep looking," said a frantic Felix as the footsteps of approaching doom neared. The old oak door creaked open. The Brethren monks entered in pairs. Big smiles on their faces belied their intentions. Jack leapt into action. Felix was getting fed up of the sound of clashing swords but he figured he would have to get used to it. His eyes caught a glimpse of something strange. On a high shelf was a model of a red British post-box. He climbed onto the table and grabbed it. "I've got it!" he screamed at Tom, throwing the model down to his thankful friend.

"Go! And good luck!" shouted Jack.

"Cheers," replied Tom.

Felix knew this would be the last time they would see Jack. Sadly Felix nodded his goodbye. He put the post-box on the floor, grabbed hold of Tom and jumped up in the air. The shudder that went up his spine shook his brain. He listened - no whistling wind, just the sound of a sword fight. They were still there. They had broken some cardinal's money box and sent coins all over the cobbled floor.

"Idiot!" shouted Tom, "we've had these since Victorian times. Keep looking."

"I haven't got it!" Felix shrieked at a more than busy Jack.

Jack laughed. "Keep going, I'm fine." He defended himself and the boys from the Brethren's blows. "Look for something obvious," he shouted.

Felix stood on the spot and scanned the room. There it was, he must have been blind! Sat in the corner was a chilled water dispenser complete with plastic cups. Tom had decided to take a cup and was sat drinking on the floor next to the machine. Felix could not remember seeing one of those in any war films he had watched.

"You ever seen one of those before?" he asked Jack pointing at the machine and Tom.

"Never, off you go," he said once again.

Jack smiled at Felix. Felix winked and ran straight into the water container, rugby tackling Tom as he ran. The boys passed out.

25

The familiar rainbow vortex greeted them when they came to. They had no idea whether this would work. The pair thought that they could end up anywhere. They desperately hoped that they would see their friends and family soon, but there was still an element of doubt.

Emile had told them that they would get back just before the time they had left. Mr Taylor would get a slap for diving out of the window like a frightened cat thought Tom.

"What if the Brethren are waiting?" he shouted to Felix.

Felix laughed as he thought that he could always create their own groundhog day by diving into the picture of Normandy in 1944 and starting the adventure over and over again.

"I think they'll be gone," said a hopeful Felix. He remembered Emile telling him that everyone would have no memory of anything that had happened after the appearance of the Brethren, and that any Guardians and Keepers killed would have disappeared.

Although they had only had a short time together Felix liked Emile. He was a kind, brave young man who thought of others before himself. Felix had once been described like that by his Scout Leader. That must be it! When one Keeper dies the next is a man of similar character in close proximity. He had just happened to be in the room when The Sheriff was about to die, so the Book chose him. Talk about wrong place at the wrong time or was it right place at the right time? Felix could not quite decide which yet.

"Relax and enjoy the ride," he laughed at Tom.

They once again passed out.

26

Felix opened his eyes slowly, hoping for the best. Delighted he found himself sat in a Geography room, G11. He was in his normal seat in his full school uniform, and sat next to him was a beaming Tom. He checked his phone - January 18th, just before 3.30 p.m., full signal. They were back, fifteen minutes before they had left. They both waited for The Sheriff to appear from the store room at the front of the classroom. A booming voice shouted, "When I come out that work needs to be finished!" It was not Mr Law. It was a short, young teacher with a shaved head and round professor like glasses. Felix looked down at his work book - he was halfway through a set of questions about sand dunes. He chuckled to himself. He'd had experience of sand dunes he did not want again. He reached inside his blazer. There, still tucked safely in his pocket was The Book of Words.

"Who the hell is this?" whispered Tom

"Matthews! That's a detention for you tomorrow night," screeched their new teacher.

The lesson finished quickly and the class were ushered off to a special assembly.

"Why are we here?" Felix asked Tom. Tom looked out from under his floppy black fringe and replied, "Apparently, according to Curly, it's a memorial service for The Sheriff and old man Buckley. Law was knocked off his bike and killed and Buckley just keeled over with a heart attack while he was sweeping in the hall."

"Right," said Felix with a stony face.

Emile had been correct. The Keeper and the Guardian had gone – with mundane everyday explanations for their deaths.

The boys knew better, but they couldn't tell anybody. The whole school spent the next hour listening to the virtues of these two men. Brave was a word that was not mentioned once. The Sheriff's war record was mentioned briefly, followed by a short prayer and the school song before the children were dismissed.

All Felix could think about was the location of the sword. He needed to find it, and find it quickly. If the Brethren turned up he would be defenceless. Tom flicked his ear playfully and said his usual line, "Footie, common now."

"We need to find the Keeper's sword," pleaded Felix.

"You planning on a scrap tonight?" quipped Tom.

Felix shrugged, and the boys spent the next hour kicking a football around with their mates on the local common. They enjoyed coming back to normality, even if it was only for a while. The only immediate danger was a sliding tackle into an unnoticed pile of dogs' mess.

Felix and Tom walked home to Felix's modern detached house with its manicured lawn. He had never been so happy to get there. Tom turned on the TV and Felix turned on the console. As Felix removed his blazer and flung it onto the sofa, the Book fell to the floor.

"The Book of Words," Felix said without thinking.

"The Sheriff's Book of Words," Tom chortled.

An hour of FIFA on the games station ensued before Felix's mum announced that tea was ready. He could not believe his eyes. On the kitchen table lay a buffet of bread, ham and a selection of cheeses! The boys laughed out loud as memories of their French diet came flooding back. Felix's mother smiled and walked out as she thought they had completely lost their marbles. The good friends did what all teenagers do and slumped upstairs in Felix's bedroom. Felix lay on the bed and Tom buried himself in a bright red scatter cushion. Tom grabbed the Book and flicked through the blank pages.

"We have to find out more about this," he said holding the Book out towards Felix.

"I know but how? We've got to get the sword first just in case The Brethren come again." Felix knew the sword would kill the monks.

"Tomorrow," said a very tired Tom. "At least let's have one decent night's sleep in our own beds."

"See you in the morning," laughed Tom. "Dad's been at his fencing club and he's picking me up at the end of the road in two minutes."

"See you tomorrow," yawned Felix and within minutes he was fast asleep.

27

Breakfast seemed dull after all of the rushed affairs before venturing out into the unknown during their seven days in France. Soon Felix was ready for school. He was just waiting for the daily knock from Tom before they wound their way to Queen Anne's School. Tom arrived and began poking fun at Felix's being special, and having the gift of travelling into the past using a magic book.

"I am History man!" he shouted as he dived over a garden wall with his hand outstretched like Superman.

Felix ignored the jibes of his best friend and followed the advice of his grandfather. He just smiled and nodded at Tom. For the rest of the walk Felix had one thing on his mind. He had to find his sword. He wondered where to start looking.

He did not have to wait long. Felix had been doing well in school, and every month the top performing students were summoned to Wonky Donkey's office for a pat on the back and a well done. Wonky Donkey was the nickname earned by their aged headmaster. His head always leaned right when he was happy, and if it leaned to the left you knew you were in trouble. For the first time ever Felix had the call. He was happy because his father had promised him he could go on the school ski trip next year if his grades improved.

Felix arrived at the office tucked away behind the main reception. A line of other smiling students had already formed. When his time came he entered the opulent office. Wonky had furnished his office like an old board room. Pictures of previous headmasters stared down at Felix. Felix scanned the shelves of trophies and strange ornaments that the school had accumulated over its long history. One trophy captured his attention most. Inside a glass case right over Wonky Donkey's head was a large bejewelled sword. A gold plaque below it read:

In Memory Of

TREVOR LAW (THE SHERIFF)

Geography Master 1949-2014

It was here - The Keepers Sword - *his* sword. He accepted his pat on the back from Wonky and rushed back to his seat in the Maths lesson.

"Here he is! Mr Smarty Pants!" Tom laughed along with the rest of the class.

Red faced, Felix turned to Tom, "I've found it, I've found The Sheriff's sword. It's in Wonky's office."

"How are we going to get it?" asked Tom "His office is always locked."

Felix shrugged and got on with his Maths. Tom was distracted and said that he felt unwell. He had felt his temperature rising since being at Felix's house. Tom put his hand up and was given permission to go to the sick bay. He was sent home later that morning. Felix had never known Tom to be ill; perhaps time travel didn't agree with him.

Felix texted his friend at lunch but there was no answer. He found a quiet corner and took the Book out from beneath his blazer. There was the school at the centre of the map. Dotted around he could see three red swords. The Guardians were making themselves ready to defend him if needed. He would go and find them that evening as he didn't have Tom to kick the football around with on the way home.

The afternoon lessons dragged on and on. The end of school bell could not come soon enough. Felix ran up the winding school drive and onto the small common. He sat on his usual bench and opened the Book to the map. The routes to the

Guardians were there marked in yellow lines. The closest marker was back in the school grounds. He remembered what Jack had told him about the sword being passed from father to son. The first sword must be young Mr Buckley who had also taken over from his father as caretaker at the school. Felix decided to talk to him tomorrow.

The second Guardian was about a mile away on the High Street. Felix wanted a snack. He would call in the supermarket near the High Street and then find him. He looked at the map again - the Guardian appeared to be in the hospital. He set off towards the other end of the common and the High Street, which was filled with schoolchildren chomping on recently purchased crisps, chocolate and gum. He checked the map to make sure it was the hospital that was his target.

28

Suddenly, a familiar sound filled the air. The council workmen's shed was in flames. Young Mr Buckley would be mad, as he borrowed the mowers to cut the school fields. The smoke began creeping across the common. Dreading what was about to appear, Felix ran to a small copse and crouched behind a gorse bush. The four monks appeared, swords drawn ready for the fight. The map showed the red swords closing in on him - the Guardians were coming. The explosion had summoned them to their duty.

Felix felt a tap on his shoulder. He burst out laughing when he turned around. There stood a stooped, grey haired figure in a long nightgown wielding a silver sabre. He was at least ninety years of age.

"My ears haven't been burning for years," he shouted.

"I'll be fine," said Felix, "go back to your bed."

"I've got weeks to live. May as well end it on my terms," he smiled.

"Anyway the evil monsters blew up my house near the school last week, they're going to get some when I get over there," the old man added.

Felix shook his hand and thanked him. He could not help thinking that everyone he came into contact with had died at the hand of the Brethren. The Sheriff, Mr Buckley, Jack, Leon and Jean-Claude were all gone. Another familiar voice rang in Felix's ears. "There are three of us now, it's almost even."

Felix spun around to see Tom's father, Gordon, glaring at the monks with a sabre ready for action.

"Get your sword out Felix, you can do this!" whispered Gordon.

"It's at school in Wonky's office!" Felix said worriedly.

The old man smiled and winked. "Take him, I'll hold them off as long as I can." He rolled up his dragging nightgown and ran as fast as he could towards the advancing monks. Once again Felix was fleeing with the sound of grating metal behind him. Gordon led him through the copse. They dashed out on to the common behind the ongoing battle. The old man was putting up a good fight, but they knew it was only a matter of time before they became the Brethren's next prey.

They were breathless when they reached the school drive. Felix was aware that they were being followed closely by a small shadowy figure. He jumped to the conclusion that the Brethren must have scouts who find the Keeper for them. They would have to deal with that later. Right now they had to get his sword! The pair burst into Wonky's office. The School Governors were half way through their meeting and watched in silent condemnation as Gordon strode across to Wonky's desk and opened the glass case.

Felix took the sword in his hand and ran to the door shouting, "Sorry sir, but I need this more than you!" Gobsmacked, Wonky sat there with his mouth wide open and his head to the left.

Gordon led Felix away from the school and back to the common. "It's best to take them on in the open. They can't corner us."

"It'll be my first fight," announced Felix in a flap.

Gordon looked worried. To their surprise the old man was still battling the monks. He had wounds all over his body but he fought on bravely. There was another figure involved in the scrap. It was Young Buckley. Felix and Gordon ran as fast as they could to join in the fray. The old man dropped to the floor, his duty done. Gordon called to Young Buckley. He retreated to form a line with Felix and Gordon. They stood like the three musketeers, together against their foe.

The monks lunged at them but the threesome remembered their training and defended until an opportunity arose for attack. The Brethren were fearsome and Felix was tiring very quickly when his first chance came. A monk swung an almighty head shot at him, he ducked below the oncoming blade and thrust his hefty weapon up into the creature's midriff. The monk sank to the floor in agony. The skin and muscle on the monster's human side melted away and the remaining bones fell into a pile at Felix's feet. Jack had told him his sword alone could kill the Brethren, and he was right.

Felix rushed to Gordon's aid. He was on the floor defenceless. His sword had been knocked out of his hand. Felix blocked what would have been a fatal blow and swung his sword round and onto the back of Gordon's assailant. Another pile of bones lay on the common as Felix helped Gordon to his feet. Gordon retrieved his sabre and re-joined the fight. Buckley was bravely battling two monks. Felix embedded his sword in the back of one of them. "Only one to go." he thought. Felix turned to see Gordon backed against a tree. Felix's fatal blow hit as the monk drove his sabre into Gordon's chest.

"Noooooooooooo!" came the shriek from the dark copse.

Tom staggered out from the shadows towards his father. Gordon held the sabre towards Tom and gasped his final words, "It's your turn now." Sobbing uncontrollably Tom took the sabre and fell to his knees next to his father's body.

29

Tom was inconsolable. Felix and Buckley helped him back to Buckley's caretaker's cottage.

"My father spent all afternoon telling me about The Guardians and their duty. My temperature was the first time I had felt the ear burning."

"I'm so sorry," sobbed Felix, feeling his best friend's pain. "I should have saved him."

"Don't be sorry. I knew this would come but I wasn't expecting it to be after a few hours." Tom said tearfully. The two best friends hugged; their bond would be stronger than ever from now on. Buckley brought them both a mug of hot tea. Having lost his father to The Brethren the previous week, he sympathised with Tom.

"We will protect you the best we can," said Tom with a brave smile.

"We'll fight them together you mean," winked Felix. He would not let these two go without a fight now he had his sword. "I need to find out about the history of The Book of Words and why The Brethren want it," Felix stated determinedly.

"That can wait," said Buckley. "He needs to go home."

Felix and Tom walked home slowly carrying their swords loosely in their hands.

"We can't walk round school with these on our belts." Tom knew they had to carry the swords but didn't know how to hide them from the other students.

"No, we'll have to wear long coats," laughed Felix.

"And look like right weirdoes!" chortled Tom.

"You have a point," said Felix with a grin.

Silently they both began addressing the problem.

"I've got it," squealed Tom. "Buckley hides his in his broom, we can hide ours in something we can carry"

"Good thinking, but what," asked Felix.

"Our guitar cases," beamed Tom.

The pair had taken up playing the instrument in primary school, and they now were part of the school rock society. Nobody would bat an eyelid at the sight of the pair carrying guitars around school. When they reached Tom's home they hid the swords in the garden shed and Felix walked Tom to the door where he was met by a tearful Mrs Matthews.

"What's wrong mum?" asked Tom pretending he was clueless as to his father's fate.

"It's your father," she sobbed. "He's had an accident."

"Not the one on the common?" asked Tom. "We passed it on our way home."

"He's been hit by a lorry," she croaked, "he was pushing an old man out of its way but they were both hit and killed."

The realisation of the evening's events hit the boys like a train and they both hugged Mrs Matthews in floods of tears. They knew the truth but somehow the book had hidden it from the world. Felix made everyone some tea. He knew this may not be the last bad news Mrs Matthews could receive at the hands of the Brethren. He promised himself that he would find a way to protect his friend and end all this nonsense. Tom did not ask for this any more than he had asked to be the Keeper. He said his goodbyes, collected his sword and slowly made his way home.

30

The front page of the local paper was filled with the story of the tragic accident on the common. It spoke of the brave hero who had given his life to try and save others. Felix smiled as he knew Gordon had given his life for more than just his fellow Guardian. He did not know exactly what, but it was bigger than the Brethren and the Book, of that he was sure.

"This is awful," said his mum.

"I know, Tom was in bits last night and so was Mrs Matthews," reported Felix.

"I'll go round and see her later, see if she needs anything," she said kindly.

Surprisingly, there was a knock at the door at the usual time, and there stood Tom with his guitar case on his back. He looked as if he had not slept a wink.

"You should be at home!" said Felix.

"I have a new job, it would a pity to be late on my first day," replied Tom with a smile. Felix put his arm around his friend, slung his guitar on his back and they set off for school.

Everyone kept their distance from the pair, not knowing what to say to Tom. He was taken to the Head of Year's office and spoken to about how to cope with his grief, but he returned to lessons fairly quickly.

"My mum says we have to get back to normal as fast as we can. Dad had told her our secret years ago but she didn't believe him until last night."

"She must be worried sick about you," Felix sympathised as he was too, knowing that the next time he would meet those creatures Tom was honour bound to protect him.

"She understood and told me to be careful. I'm having a fencing lesson tonight. Want to come?" Tom asked Felix.

"May as well," said Felix. "We know it will come in handy."

The day continued as any normal school day. All students in Year 8 were given a letter to take home. There was to be a talk as part of their Religious Education lessons from an old Jewish gentlemen, a survivor of the holocaust during the Second World War. Felix's mind immediately turned to Emile. The last time he had seen him he was about to be loaded onto a boat and shipped off to a death camp.

Felix felt guilty. He could not leave Emile there to die at the hands of the German gas chambers. On the way home Felix was feeling low. Tom tried cheering him up with jokes and gossip but nothing worked.

"I have to go back," said Felix excitedly. "I have to save Emile from this!" he said waving the letter in Tom's face. Tom suddenly realised where the Germans were taking Emile and his family.

"How can you go back?" Tom blurted out. "And who's going to look after you? All the Guardians are dead."

"There is someone," said Felix "Trevor."

"Trevor? He's just a soldier, he can't fight the Brethren!" shouted Tom, "I'm coming with you and don't try and stop me. I'm your Guardian now!"

Felix grabbed him by the arm and they ran back to Felix's house. Felix shouted, "Mum, we've got a project on Paris to do. Where are dad's photos and booklets?"

"In the shoebox under his desk," came the helpful reply.

The pair bounded up the stairs and into the study. They emptied the shoebox onto the floor. Felix grabbed a photo of the Eiffel Tower showing his dad and his drunk mates on rugby tour. He checked he had the Book and sword and placed the photo in a clearing amongst the mess. He smiled at Tom and jumped into the air. Tom pushed his friend onto the chair.

"What are you doing?" screamed Felix.

"How the hell are we going to get back to here? I'm coming too" said Tom. "You'll need my help. It'll take time to find the object and you don't know where it will be, we may not have that long to search."

Remembering the journey from Berlin, Felix took out his mobile and took a photo of the room.

"There!" he said, "sorted!"

Without warning, Felix pushed Tom out of the room and jumped onto the photo of his dad. By the time Tom ran back into the room, Felix had disappeared.

Felix felt safe in the rainbow vortex as he travelled, and he waited for the sudden thump when he arrived at his destination. He came round and heard singing. He opened his eyes and there stood his dad and his mates singing rugby songs. He was in Paris, but it was 1988 not 1944. He had needed a photo form June 1944 to get to Emile. He laughed at the drunken idiots staggering towards the Tower, placed his mobile on the floor and jumped into it. He was on his way back home. He opened his eyes hoping he was on the floor of the study.

Tom was livid. "All done?" he asked angrily.

"Wrong time," said Felix with a smile. "Where are the books on Paris? We need a picture of 1944."

"Dad told me about a memorial to the Jews who were shipped from Paris. There's a tunnel under Notre Dame filled with candles. One for each of the people taken from there. I don't want Emile to be a candle!" screamed Felix as he frantically threw papers everywhere. Together they searched through the pile on the floor.

"Here it is!" screeched Tom, handing Felix a leaflet. On the front cover was a picture of the memorial. But that was no good - they would end up in the time when the photo was taken. He opened the leaflet and there it was - June 12th 1944, a picture of the loading of the prisoners. He threw it on the floor and grabbed his phone, sword and the Book. Before he could jump, Tom knocked him onto the chair.

"How are we going to get back?" said a worried Tom, jogging Felix's memory.

Felix laughed and held up his phone to take a photo of the room. Quickly, he jumped into the photo shouting, "Sorry mate, I can't let you come." Tom hurled himself forward and grabbed hold of Felix just in time. The pair passed out once again.

31

The vortex journey was filled with trepidation. This time they really were on a mission. This was not about the Book, this was personal. They woke up on the bridge looking down on the shipping dock alongside Notre Dame. Tom was kneeling over Felix with that stupid big grin on his face.

"What did you do that for?" whispered Felix.

"I told you, I'm your Guardian. You're not going anywhere without me," Tom said bravely. He added, "Anyway, you're the only one that can kill these things, so if you think I'm fighting them without you, you can think again." Felix knew he couldn't talk Tom out of it. It was late evening. The clock on a church said half past seven. They were early. The pair made their way to Trevor's safe house.

Disbelief was the only way to describe Trevor's face when he saw the boys at the door.

"What in the name of all that is good are you doing back here?"

"We've come to save Emile," said Felix.

"Jack died to get you home and you stand there wanting to save Emile." Trevor was very angry.

"We have to," pleaded Felix, before telling Trevor what they had seen before his journey home and what it meant for Emile.

"You've brought your sword this time then," Trevor quipped.

"You never know who will be there," said Felix.

"I've got mine too!" screamed Tom waving his sabre around like Zorro.

"Who in God's name gave him a sword?" laughed Trevor, "They must be bonkers!"

The peace of the evening was shattered by a distant explosion. The Brethren had arrived. Trevor threw the boot polish to the boys along with some old clothes and a rucksack. They once again stuffed their uniforms into the sack and the trio set off into the gloomy evening light. They weaved in and out of the lanes past many familiar buildings until they reached the street on which Emile had been placed in a safe house. There in full view he was being dragged into an open back truck along with his mother, who was carrying what must have been Emile's toddler brother. The truck departed for the shipping dock.

"Where is Emile Dupont?" came a gravelly voice from behind them.

Trevor turned and let rip with his machine gun, but the bullets went straight through the monks with no effect on their wellbeing.

"Leave this to us," shouted Tom as if he'd been doing this all his life. He pushed passed Trevor and lunged at the first monk. Felix drew his sword and in a short and swift fight in the confined space there were soon four piles of bones. Smiling broadly Trevor quipped, "You've come on a tad in the last 70 years!" The three of them sat there laughing for a moment taking in what the two teenagers had just accomplished.

They ran down to the river and headed towards the bridge.

"How are we going to save him?" whispered Felix. Trevor came to an abrupt stop next to a small rowing boat.

"Jump in," he murmured. The boat hugged the river bank as Tom and Trevor slowly rowed towards Notre Dame. They could see the truck unloading the people from Emile's neighbourhood. Felix tapped Trevor on the back and pointed at the unfolding scene. Trevor nodded and began rowing towards the barge that the Jews were being crammed onto. There were four guards and two people in the wheelhouse.

"I'll sort the wheelhouse, you take the guards once we're underway." Trevor wished them good luck and left the boys.

Tom climbed up the side of the barge, pulling Felix up behind him. They slipped onto the crowded deck and hid amongst the families who clutched their belongings and children close to them. Emile and his family were thrown onto the barge. They huddled in a corner and Emile's mother started wailing like a lot of the other frightened women. Felix and Tom crept slowly over to Emile. Felix placed his hand over Emile's mouth. Emile turned ready to fight but smiled when he saw Felix.

"What are you doing here?" the French boy whispered excitedly.

"I know where this boat is going. We've come back to get you off it," said Felix.

"No!" whimpered Emile "The second rule of the Book."

"What rules?" said Tom sharply. "Nobody said anything about any rules. I never follow them anyway," he added defiantly.

"When you go home get Felix to ask the Book," Emile replied as he reached for his sword. It was gone. Felix pulled back his coat to reveal the Keeper's weapon.

"Future Keeper wins again," laughed Felix.

He gave Emile a knife and pointed to the guards at the rear of the barge. Emile nodded in unspoken understanding. Five minutes after the barge set off there were two loud splashes quickly followed by two more. Felix looked in the wheelhouse. Trevor winked at him. Two gagged Germans lay at his feet. The barge moved slowly and elegantly up the River Seine gliding through the shimmering summer moonlight.

"Well this is romantic," said Tom, "a trip up the Seine by moonlight." In the wheelhouse the four of them got the giggles.

Once they had left the city Trevor moored the barge. He told the confused crowd that they were free. There was a loud cheer. Some grabbed their belongings and disappeared into the dark countryside. Many decided to carry on in the barge up the river and try to get to England and safety. Emile waved to his mother and younger brother as they sailed away into the night.

"Best get you home again," said Trevor to the beaming teenagers who had just saved hundreds of people from certain death.

"Easy this time," Felix replied as he pulled out his phone. "What will you do now?"

"I'll help the resistance disrupt the German retreat," said Emile with great enthusiasm. "Trevor says he needs a new partner."

Felix threw his phone on the floor.

"Right Monsieur Law let's find some mischief," Emile said to Trevor.

"Trevor Law?" shouted Tom as the penny dropped and he smiled at Felix.

"Yes, why?" asked Trevor.

"No reason. Thank you and good bye," shouted Felix as he jumped into his phone, Tom's arms firmly hung around his chest.

Trevor and Emile shrugged their shoulders and began the long walk back to Paris.

32

Felix was shaken back to life by Tom.

"Well" he said.

"Glad that's done, I couldn't sleep if we hadn't gone back," smiled Felix.

He opened the Book and looked at the list of Keepers.

"Why are you staring at a blank page?"

"It's not blank, you just can't see it!" exclaimed Felix.

"It's not changing" said Felix dully, "He still dies in 1944."

Disappointedly, he slammed the Book shut and threw it against the wall. Tom left silently to get refreshments.

"Why does he still die?" Felix asked the Book.

He opened it to the second page. There the answer came:

'There are rules dear boy. You cannot break the rules.'

"What are the stupid rules?" he shouted. He was angry that his last journey was pointless.

Rule 1	The power is honest. Only use the book for what you think is right and not for personal gain.
Rule 2	You cannot change events in time.
Rule 3	Ask the right questions on your quest and you will get helpful advice.
Rule 4	Only one book and sword can work at one time.
Rule 5	Seven days is all you have before time will end your reign as Keeper.
Rule 6	The rest you will figure out as you go.

He began to understand why the date on the list had not changed. He also understood how The Sheriff knew so much. He just had one unanswered question. What had happened to Emile?

33

They still did not quite believe that they could travel through time. Felix wanted to put the Book out of his mind for a few days. He hid it under his mattress and went about his business of school and play. The day finally came of the Holocaust survivor's lecture. Tom and Felix were looking forward to it, but they had been warned by Miss Barker that the content might upset them and that there was no shame in crying. Tom had also been warned repeatedly that his humour would not be appreciated by anyone.

Not really knowing what to expect, the whole of Year 8, all two hundred and fifty of them, were filed in and asked to sit silently in the school hall. Young Buckley was stood at the light switches and waved at Felix and Tom. They waved back, embarrassed, through the mocking stares of the students in front of them.

Mrs Barker climbed up the steep wooden steps at the side of the stage and approached the microphone. She gave instructions on how they were to behave. There would be no whooping and hollering and no rhythmic clapping. The usual warning that usually ended up in rhythmic clapping! The lights were dimmed and the assembled crowd stood to welcome Wonky Donkey and a small grey haired gentleman with a large handlebar moustache. He was smartly dressed in a shirt, tie, blue blazer and grey trousers. They slowly made their way towards the stage. The old man was helped up onto the stage and was introduced to the expectant crowd. He spent the first half an hour giving a history of Jewish persecution during the war. The students were sat silently, every pair of eyes and ears focussed on the slideshow and every word out of the old man's mouth. The children felt every emotion possible. Guilt, happiness, sadness, shame, joy came and went.

The second half of the talk concentrated on the man's personal story. He had grown up in Paris. He talked of German searches and people disappearing. He showed slides of people being loaded onto barges outside Notre Dame. Then he told an amazing story of three heroes who had captured a barge and sailed away up the River Seine to freedom. He had made it to England with his mother and had lived here ever since. He then put up a photo of the rescuers. On the twenty foot square screen behind him was a grainy photograph of Trevor, Emile, Felix and Tom all with big cheesy grins on their boot polished faces. Nearly every student and teacher turned to look at Felix and Tom. They both shrugged and laughed, realising that this man was Mr Dupont, Emile's younger brother. The man finished with an emotional story of how his brother had stayed to help the resistance fight the Germans but had unfortunately been killed whilst trying to blow up a bridge with Trevor. Instead of being killed by the Nazis or Brethren, he had been killed fighting for freedom. His big brother Emile was his hero. Emile had died ten days after the rescue. Tom looked at Felix and winked. Felix was relieved in a strange way that Emile had enjoyed his last days. It also explained how the book had been passed on to The Sheriff. He had been there when Emile had died.

There were tears everywhere and tissues were being distributed by the teachers who were also weeping.

34

Weeks flew by with no incident and the boys worked hard towards their end of year exams. There had been no sign of the Brethren, and Felix and Tom were closer than ever. Both took fencing lessons and their skills grew every week. They practised religiously every day in Tom's garage where he had rigged up swinging bags and sticks for them to fight against.

The exams were taken during normal lesson slots and were hard work. They had gone well until today. Both were dreading the History test. They loved History but they had difficulty remembering facts and dates as well as the names. This could prove problematic in a History test.

They chatted on the way to school, going through the list of Kings and Queens. They talked through the chapters of world history they had studied, but their memories were hazy. They filed into Mr Taylor's classroom. Felix and Tom always giggled as they entered his lessons, knowing how much of a coward this hulk of a man had been in the face of the Brethren. The expectant students all politely said thank you as they received their test papers. They waited for those immortal words, "You have one hour. You may begin."

Tom turned over the first page and looked straight at Felix. The look of panic on his face reflected his own feelings. "Do you know any of this?" he mouthed to his friend.

"No, none of it!" whispered Felix.

"What are we going to do?" said a fraught Felix.

"I have one idea." Tom took The Book of Words from Felix's bag.

"No!" laughed Felix as he realised what Tom was planning, "We can't..."

With a look of mischief on his face, Felix stood up on the desk and drew his sword from his guitar case, much to the amusement of his classmates and the horror of Mr Taylor. Tom drew his own sword and joined Felix on the desk. Felix bent down and opened the booklet to a large picture, and the pair linked arms and jumped onto the exam paper.

Felix and Tom were gone.

Join Felix on his next adventure...

Felix Jones and The Honour of the Keeper

A Felix Jones Adventure

Felix Jones is The Keeper of The Book of Words. The Brethren's search for The Book brings danger and adventure to Felix and his best friend Tom. Determined to end The Keeper's age old enemies' quest for power, the boys travel back to the Dark Ages in search of the first Keeper, hoping he can provide the answers they seek. The Book and Merlin teach them important lessons of the responsibility Felix now has if he is to fulfil his role as The Keeper.

Printed in Great Britain
by Amazon.co.uk, Ltd.,
Marston Gate.